Nathaniel
& the
Midnight Movers

a novel

Nathaniel & the Midnight Movers

a novel

J. Ronald M. York

Nathaniel & the Midnight Movers

J. Ronald M. York
p. cm.

MANUFACTURED IN THE UNITED STATES OF AMERICA

ISBN 978-0-9982734-7-1

This book is printed on acid-free paper.

First Edition

visit www.JRonaldMYork.com

Acknowledgments

This book would not have been possible without the
help and guidance from

Mary Helen Clarke, Ralph Henley, Trish Luna,
Rebecca Pierce, Lynette Sesler & Julie Schoerke

Cover illustration and concept by
Arden von Haeger

Author photo by
Larry Ray

Chapter One
present day

"Excuse me. Could you tell me a little something about this table?"

I thought to myself that I can't remember the backstories for all of my pieces, and often find that after so many years and so many episodes that I have become occasionally forgetful and easily confused. But you can be assured that everything of mine comes with an interesting provenance.

My moving sale had begun nearly two hours earlier than advertised, thanks to those damn "Early Bird" shoppers. Neighbors and strangers were anxious to offer diddly-squat for my assorted collectables. You see, I had finally reached the point of no longer wanting the biggest and best now that my Medicare birthday was fast approaching. I felt that it was time to downsize, not only in square footage but in furnishings as well.

My arthritic knees no longer enjoyed climbing the stairs to my bedroom. The extravagant, over-the-top clutter that I had surrounded myself with for so long felt suffocating. Previously it had given me joy but now I no longer felt the need to entertain the pretentious queens I had called friends at one time. Some of them have died, others are in poor health and yet a few still struggled to keep up appearances. However, makeup and soft lighting cannot completely disguise the wrinkles and dated wardrobes. And believe me, thirty-plus years ago they would not have been caught dead driving a decade old economy car.

Presentation was everything. "Fake it till you make it" was our motto even if it left many drowning in debt.

Let's face it, my ragtag group of friends and acquaintances had gotten old. Most could not or would not try to keep up with fashion trends or the latest designers. And do not even get me started on technology. Of course, there were always those who would continue to pretend that they were still in their prime and had the finances to impress the type of young men who only saw dollar signs and not the aging hand of the one who wrote their generous checks. And yes, even I would have loved for someone older to have been philanthropic to me when I was a pretty young thing. But now it just seemed sort of sad.

My moving sale was in full swing and fortunately, I had hired the professional team from Roberta Ann's Trash & Treasures Estate Sales to organize and price everything. Roberta Ann and the girls were on hand to host the event as well. They had worried that it would make me sad seeing my possessions hauled away and suggested that it might be best if I did not hang around. But actually, I felt free. Not only was I getting rid of the clutter, but I also was saying goodbye to the past which often had me fearful of being caught, arrested and hauled off to jail. In fact, I had always wondered if the statute of limitations would expire before I did.

Folding tables were set up inside and out to display small items and linens. Some pieces of furniture had been moved outside because it appeared that the weather had decided to cooperate. I absolutely refused to have my entire home open to the unwashed masses and yet, three rooms had so much in them that it was just easier to remove my personal items and leave the furniture, lamps and art as they were. And since some of the girls were watching over the interior as well as having some doors shut with signs saying "Do Not Enter," I decided to grab a lawn chair, find a spot under the shade of my constantly shedding magnolia tree and enjoy the show.

—•—

"I said, excuse me, I was asking if you could tell me anything about this table?" she repeated herself.

A smile came to my face. For a brief moment, I thought back to when and how that piece was procured.

"Yes, I believe that I can," I replied.

The whiny voice asking the question belonged to a too skinny, Botoxed, bleached blond woman in painted-on yoga pants. She was one of several that morning rummaging through the baubles offered in my moving sale. I wanted to tell her that her yoga pants were the equivalent of body paint – basically hiding nothing. But instead, with a sincere smile on my face, I began to tell this swizzle stick of a woman the history of the table. Well, let's say, a <u>version</u> of the history according to me, Ricky, the award-winning successful interior designer. As opposed to the other me, the thief-in-the-night Nathaniel.

"Oh, my dear, that is one of my favorite pieces. It breaks my heart to let it go, but I just don't have room in my new place," I said with false sincerity. "I bought that piece new over 40 years ago at Palmer's Fine Furniture. Do you remember that store? They carried only the best of the best," I continued knowing that I had her full attention.

"Oh yes, my parents used to shop there when I was a child, but it was long gone by the time I was ready to furnish my first home," she said – as if she actually believed that.

I thought to myself that maybe her face looked young enough to pull off that lie but the age spots on her spindly arms led me to think she was a good twenty years older than she was imagining herself to be. An aging trophy wife trying desperately not to be replaced.

Regardless, I was just as adept at lying as she was and anxious to sell her a piece or two.

"I fell in love with that table and knew it would be a wonderful complement in my room. It was also the favorite of the one who eventually broke my heart – which has made it a painful reminder over the years. I have had such conflicted feelings in loving this table but still seeing it connected to the hurt that had been inflicted upon me," I said as I spread it on thick and creamy.

"Oh my, I am so sorry. I did not mean to make you relive painful memories," she tried to convey with concern.

"No, I am the one who should be sorry. You do not need to know all of that nonsense. All you need to know is that it is a beautiful and well-loved table offered at a ridiculously affordable price simply because, for me, it has always been a reminder of a difficult period in my life," I said, coming in for the home run.

I could tell that she was trying to show sympathy on her face but with everything frozen in time, all she could do was pull off that startled, surprised look, which can happen from too much "refreshening" by a plastic surgeon.

"It is a good price and you know, I feel that I should buy it just so you can move on without this constant reminder of a tragic love," she said, as I was mentally congratulating myself and thinking that my performance was worthy of a curtain call.

"Thank you, my dear. Cash or check?"

Chapter Two
1970s

Someone once told me that if you want to tell a convincing lie, you need to stick closely to the truth. That sage advise has served me well. You see, I worked at a small gift shop in a boring retail job during the day. "Yes, that throw pillow would be a wonderful accent on your lovely (nasty, lumpy, out-of-style) sofa." "Of course, those silver frames would be perfect sitting on your bookshelves with photos of your beautiful (with faces only a mother could love) children."

In retail, you always want to make the customer happy which involves telling them what they want to hear, even if it is a lie. Now, as a thief, when someone asks me where I bought something, I find that telling them that I broke into a house in their neighborhood and stole it tends to set off alarms. So, I have learned to tell a convincing lie.

Already I am sure you have formed an opinion of me. I mean, when you hear the word "thief," it is hard to focus on anything else. But there is so much more to me.

I never set my goals in life to be the successful boss of a local crime ring – any more than I had planned on being the school mascot or a waiter at a theme park or a part-time drag queen. Things just happen – after all, I am a multitasker. Of course, now that I think about it, they were all connected in that I was *pretending to be someone else*.

I am almost 6' tall, average weight, okay, maybe a pound or two heavy. But I have heard that I am thought of as attractive or handsome. I also have thick wavy dark blonde "surfer" hair – one of my best features, and a mustache like many of the current popular actors (and porn stars, so I have been told). I was raised middle class with loving parents who worked hard to keep up with their wealthier friends. They weren't being pretentious or living a lie but with a circle of friends which seemed to have it easier than most, my parents just wanted to fit in. They made sure that I was educated with a college degree, and they nurtured my natural flair for design.

I think it was my design flair that made me want pretty things. My total lack of finances made me conclude stealing might be my only way of ever having them. I mean, as a child I would steal candy from the neighborhood market and then eventually moved up to cigarettes, which I never really took a liking to. I can't say the same for the candy, as my waistline can attest to. However, once I had my driver's license, I was able to move on to bigger, better and shinier things.

I have always loved looking at real estate. Sunday afternoons, as a child, I went on excursions with my parents checking out open houses. I was just as happy seeing the finished homes as well as those under construction. With my vivid imagination, I have a gift for seeing in my mind what a project could look like when finished. To this day, I still enjoy riding around looking at homes for sale. I love to challenge myself when viewing an older home that has lingered on the market. I like to imagine how I might improve it. I have also been guilty of looking at homes under construction and recognizing what I felt to be a distinct flaw in the floor plan and knowing that it could easily be fixed. Several times I have left anonymous notes explaining my design ideas and twice I have returned some time later to find that the contractors had altered their original plan and moved a doorway, window or whatever I had proposed. Of course, others have ignored my ideas, which left me to wonder later if they had wished they had made that simple change I had suggested, when their new home remained on the market month after month.

It was this love of exploring that allowed me to see new and wonderful things in design. Simple things such as drawer and cabinet knobs in the shape of roses, which I thought would look nice in my mother's bathroom at home – so there I am, unscrewing them and taking them with me to save for a present for her at a later date. There was also a bathroom mirror I found in one home. I felt that it was definitely a cut above what you would have expected and envisioned it at the end of our hall leading to the family bedrooms. So it too found it's way into my car and was hidden in our basement until just the right time to present as a gift.

One of those crazy coincidences happened a few years later when I started working as an interior designer. Clients in a spacious new home mentioned something about their previous residence, which turned out to be the house where I had taken the bathroom mirror. The same mirror that hung at the end of the hall in my parents' home until it was sold during the estate sale held after their deaths.

Drawer knobs, a mirror and a chandelier were some of my earliest acquisitions. And then the next logical step, furniture. A new road in our well-developed subdivision had just opened up in the late 1960s and spec houses were going up on both sides of the street. The hillside lots were spacious, allowing maximum privacy for each home. One builder, being quite proud of his completed two-story colonial-style house, partnered with Palmer's, a furniture store located downtown, to decorate it for marketing. I had looked through the windows of the home and was impressed by what I saw. I will admit that I had not planned to make much of a dent but thought that a table or two, maybe even a lamp, could find it's way into the back of my parents' car one evening.

As it turned out, it was summer and church friends were going on vacation. They asked my parents if I might be able to house sit for them. They had recently come into money, moved into a much larger home and had begun collecting antiques. Their new home felt like a museum with elaborate draperies, rugs and a pair of his and her portraits that appeared to stare you down whenever you were in the same room. And, how can I say this delicately – neither husband or wife would have won a beauty contest so these oversized, ornately framed, oil portraits would often elicit giggles and whispers among their acquaintances.

My parents thought that it would be fine for me to spend a few days house sitting for their friends during the summer of my junior year in high school. With a newly minted driver's license and one of the family cars, I was given unlimited freedom. Remember, this was 1969 when phones were still attached to walls. Parents were easier to avoid.

Our friends' home was old, dark and a bit creepy. Yes, it was impressive but also somewhat smothering with all of the newly acquired heavy antique furnishings. The house had belonged to a former car dealer who had either slipped and fell or had an attack of some sort while taking a shower and crashed through the glass shower door to his death. The door had been replaced but still it left me a tad uneasy when taking a shower. Nevertheless, staying there was quite an adventure.

So with my newfound freedom, I drove back to our neighborhood one evening around dusk and pulled my car behind the furnished model home whose windows I had peered in the week before. The houses on each side were still under construction and home alarm systems had not and would not become commonplace for several more years. I felt relatively safe as I bumped my backside again and again into the kitchen door causing it to splinter from the single lock. Unfortunately, a bit of trim came off in the process, but I hoped that it would be an easy fix.

Like a kid in a candy store, I ran from room to room seeing all of the options and hastily made a decision. I was smart enough to know that time was not on my side and that I needed to be quick. There was an octagon-shaped commode table that I liked and an elegant Hepplewhite console table as well. The console fit into the wide back seat of my family's 1969 four-door Buick LeSabre sedan. The end table was bulky and not easily moved but I was running on youthful adrenaline and managed to get it loaded into the trunk. When I went back to pull the door closed, I thought, "What the hell" and grabbed a brass lamp on my way out.

I carefully pulled out of the drive, headed down the street and felt relieved at not seeing anyone else around. I remember thinking that this house was practically in walking distance of my family home, where my parents were probably enjoying dinner in front of the TV console. Driving cautiously back to where I was staying, I unloaded my new-found treasures into the attic of our friends' home. I had my story in place by the time they had returned from their trip. I told them I had these pieces on layaway for some time and was finally able to pay them off. I also told them that they were to be a Christmas surprise for my parents and I asked if it would be okay if I stored them in their attic for the next few months.

"Aren't you just the perfect son?" said the family friends, impressed by my gesture. "Your mom and dad are so lucky."

They readily agreed to store my ill-gotten gain in their attic. On Christmas eve I picked up everything and surprised my parents the next morning with the console and commode table. I had left the brass lamp in the trunk of the Buick until they were both showering and getting dressed Christmas morning. Then I quickly slipped the lamp, which turned out to be the desirable Stiffel brand, out of the trunk and hurried upstairs and hid it in the side attic off of the playroom above our garage. I knew that it was already risky giving my parents two pieces of furniture. The lamp made it feel truly excessive. And since it was the smallest item, I figured that it would be the easiest to hide for a while.

The year before, I had placed a $99 lighted glass curio cabinet from another furniture store on layaway for payments of $10 a month. Between my allowance and grass-cutting summer jobs, I had it paid off just in time for the previous Christmas. My parents knew that story to be true. So, this year my story did not seem too far-fetched. Or, maybe they did suspect something but did not want to know or accept the truth. Of course, mom and dad knew the amount of my limited weekly allowance and they could have had a rough idea of what I had saved from cutting grass and house sitting. Still, even though it was suspect, it was almost believable enough that they allowed themselves to accept my convincing lie. Regardless, no more questions were raised and they bragged to their friends about my generosity. That was my first solo furniture run and I longed for another.

Chapter Three

In the early 1970s, I was up to my eyeballs in college studies and hijinks. My single dorm room was probably the only one "professionally" decorated (by me!), in the male dorm. I had convinced my mother to buy a rug, bedspread, draperies and a couple of framed prints to hang on the wall. Plus, I had finally taken the brass lamp from its hiding place in our attic and placed it by my twin bed. While my classmates were stealing street signs to hang on their walls, I had an expensive Stiffel brass lamp with an eggshell silk shade stolen from a furnished model home.

Having fabulous taste in a dorm environment did not come without cost. Some of the guys made fun of the sissy guy with the "girly" things but I knew that a few of them were secretly envious. And being the school mascot, a beaver, (granted, probably the gayest beaver ever) the dorm jocks had my back. I mean literally some of them, late at night, had my back, front and well... sorry, I digress.

However, by my senior year, I had moved out of the dorm and into an apartment with Dean, a classmate from school. My parents offered a few pieces of furniture and Dean and I managed to abscond with a sofa, rug and chair from an unused dorm at the school. Certainly not the quality of what I had pilfered in the past, but still respectable and a cut above what our classmates had.

Dean was a redheaded, freckled-face handsome boy who matched me in height and weight. Okay, he was maybe a little bit thinner, but still, we could share clothes. He would be gay when the occasion called for it but most of the time, he acted like he was straight. We were in several classes together at school and got along well, whether in the same bed or not. He could charm anyone with the exception of my dad, who after meeting him said, "That boy is so full of shit." I could not argue with that. Still, Dean and I had fun.

We only spent a few months in that dumpy apartment before moving into a much nicer and larger apartment across town. To be able to afford this luxury, we added another roommate from college, Greg. He was a bit shorter, but like me, his weight would sometimes fluctuate. He could weigh less but then he would balloon up and be heavier – something I have battled all of my life too. Plus, he enjoyed having his brown hair frosted because I guess you can never look too gay. Regardless, the three of us thought we had finally arrived with our new avocado-colored carpeted three-bedroom town house.

Greg had already purchased bedroom furniture from a huge new store in town. It was the early 1970s and Mediterranean-style furnishings were coming on strong. He had found a three-piece bedroom suite that appeared to be heavily carved wood but on closer inspection, the door fronts were molded plastic. To complement the style, he bought a red crushed-velvet bedspread and a swag lamp to hang over the bedside chest.

Dean decided to buy a new sofa bed. He wanted his bedroom to function as both a sitting room and bedroom. The fabric was a scratchy Herculaneum plaid in gold, rust and avocado and every bit as stylish and hideous as it sounds. An inexpensive chest of drawers and matching bookshelf completed the look. If there was any doubt that Dean was not 100% gay, it could easily be confirmed by his decorating taste.

Unfortunately, all of our fashion choices for the 1970s featured double-knit polyester clothing in bold plaids and colors. Trust me when I say that I have burned any and all photographic evidence.

I opted to pay a higher rent to get the larger master bedroom with an adjoining half-bath. Although we had another half-bath downstairs, the three us had to share the one and only bathtub located in the hall bathroom upstairs. For my bedroom, my thoughtful parents purchased a solid wood Italian provincial triple dresser, headboard and nightstand in a fruitwood finish. A couple of years later, they purchased the same bedroom furniture for themselves. I found a woven royal blue and olive patterned bedspread for my double bed. My "five-fingered discounted" brass lamp sat on my bedside nightstand.

We had legally upgraded our upstairs furnishings and that appeased me for a while. The downstairs was still a hodge-podge of collected odds and ends, including the 1940s Duncan Phyfe sofa that Dean and I had found and liberated from the closed-off dorm at school. Its gray with rose tapestry fabric actually complemented an area rug in similar colors. My parents had donated a 1950s nubby bark-cloth, beige armchair and the Formica-top kitchen table with hairpin metal legs from my youth, complete with four matching vinyl covered chairs.

My design sense tried to make the best of what we had, but I will admit that I was longing for something a little more *Architectural Digest* and a little less *Field and Stream*. Neither Dean nor Greg was aware of my "midnight-run" skills but it would not be long before they would learn and become my apprentices.

—●—

The three of us spent a year in that three-bedroom apartment and, for the most part, came out unscathed. Greg had dropped out or was invited to leave college because he was deemed "too colorful" for the tight-knit religious school. Oh, there were plenty of fine upstanding young men messing around in the dark but they were discreet – a word that was not in Greg's vocabulary. So in 1972 he basically did a twirl in his red stilettos and sashayed out of there. Dean also dropped out before graduation, leaving me as the only one in our little threesome still in school. Eventually, Dean decided that he wanted to move out. Greg and I were forced financially to take a smaller apartment a few doors down. It was in that apartment that I honed Greg's skills and slowly but surely, the home makeover began.

I still loved looking at houses. It did not matter if they were under construction or completed. Of course, it was always an added perk if they were furnished. Condominiums were all the rage and popping up in several areas around town. Realtors would entice buyers with their furnished models. One such development, Lake Manor, was already in phase two when I discovered it on a lazy Sunday afternoon.

There were four floor plans available but only two models were furnished. I avoided the unit where the salesman had an office, but I did breeze through the other model and liked what I saw. Now, you may find this hard to believe but at the time, I only wanted the draperies.

I had found rolls of wallpaper in a house under construction a couple of months earlier and had decided to tackle wallpapering our apartment kitchen. For the first time out, I did a fairly good job. However, on closer inspection you might have noticed the pattern headed downhill near the refrigerator. Still I was pleased with the addition even though it made the tacky apartment drapes covering the sliding glass doors to the patio, even more of an eyesore. I had found just what I needed and unlocked a window on my way out of the furnished model with plans to return after hours.

I returned to the complex after dark and raised the unlocked window to let myself in. Then without turning the lights on, I began to unhook the draperies. Once they were down and folded, I carried them out to my hand-me-down Buick LeSabre and stumbled over an umbrella stand on the way. I am not sure what possessed me, but I grabbed it too and tossed it into my car. Going back to lock up, I thought that the small pull-up barrel chair by the door might easily fit into my back seat, so I grabbed it too. There was so much for the taking but I feared I had overstayed my welcome.

Greg worked the front desk during the evening shift at a motel near our apartment. By the time he got home, I had the avocado and cream woven draperies hung, the antiqued gold umbrella stand by the door and the new barrel chair with ochre textured fabric placed at one end of the sofa. He could not have been more excited or curious as to where everything had come from. I decided it was time to level with him and gave him a version of what had happened while acting as if it was my first time – you know, just a spur of the moment decision.

"I want to go check it out," Greg said as he plopped down in the new chair.

Naturally seeing what I had just brought home had left him chomping at the bit and anxious to run back out there. I could not blame him for wanting to see for himself what else might be available.

"It would be too risky to return tonight. Someone may have seen or heard me and be on alert," I said, and assured him that there would be other opportunities. I warned him that it was too big of a risk to go back now.

However, this little taste of something new also had me jonesing for more – and Greg was practically bouncing from leg to leg, anxious for the opportunity to join in the fun. I was able to hold him off for a week by promising to go back out on Sunday for the next open house.

As promised, I took Greg out to Lake Manor. But other than a few small accessories stuffed in the pockets of our jackets, we did not attempt anything else. I had not realized just how many people already lived in the units adjoining the models when I was there earlier. Or how easy it would have been to spot me loading my car in the night. I felt very lucky to have gotten away with the first haul but not comfortable enough to try it again. Still, I knew there would be other options out there and with careful preparation, I was willing to start making plans for the next heist.

Chapter Four

True to my word, I found our next mark – another brand new house in the neighborhood near my family home. This one was a slick stucco contemporary multilevel number perched on a wooded hillside lot. The house had just been completed and a realtor's "for sale" sign placed in the yard. Since it was impossible to tell from the street if there was a car at the top of the drive, I had my story ready just in case I ran into someone. "Friends of mine had looked and were interested in the property." Followed with "They had asked me to run by and take a look."

Good news! There was no one waiting for me at the top of the hill. Bad news! The house was locked. Still, I looked through the windows and found that it was completely empty. While disappointing at first, it actually did allow me to focus on the luscious chocolate-brown, short-shag wall-to-wall carpet. Avocado and Harvest Gold were still strong in the 1970s but the next new thing on the design horizon appeared to be chocolate brown. And I wanted it, needed it, and had to have it!

I called Greg at work as soon as I got home and told him what I had found. He immediately began to pepper me with questions.

"Wall to wall carpet? How the hell are we going to steal carpet that's already laid down? Will it even fit in your car? And who is going to lay it for us? Are you nuts?" Greg ranted.

"Are you done, Miss Thing? I mean, seriously, girl, breathe," I patiently replied. Greg tended to overreact sometimes so I had to verbally slap him around a bit.

"Now, if you would just shut the hell up and listen. We can pull up the carpet, roll it and drag it to the car. Hopefully we can fold the roll and fit it into my trunk so that it won't hang out too much. As far as installing it, we will figure something out. I mean, you know you want it as bad as me," I said.

He agreed and then started to get excited. His work shift did not end until ten and I knew that he would be home fifteen minutes after that and ready to go. That put us driving up the steep gravel drive around eleven PM. I was grateful for the secluded wooded lot but with tires spinning in the gravel and headlights bouncing off of the trees, our arrival had been clearly announced. I knew that there were no neighbors on either side of the house but still, anyone living on that street could have seen or heard us and wondered why there was activity that late at night.

At the top of the hill I put my car in park, turned the engine off and killed the lights. We carefully opened our doors, got out, and closed them as softly as possible. It is amazing how far the slightest sound can carry in the still of the night. I had already explained to Greg that we needed to wait for just a few minutes to make sure no one heard us and decided to investigate. Waiting is often the hardest part. You always want and need to be cautious but at the same time getting in and out of a job quickly is always preferred.

"Are you sure there is not an unlocked door or window?" Greg asked. Neither one of us wanted to break down the door.

"I checked earlier today but it's worth checking again," I said hopefully.

The dark-stained wooden front door was indeed locked, as was the sliding glass door off what appeared to be the dining room. We both tried to raise the windows within our reach but with no luck. I tripped and slid on my butt as I walked down the hillside to the basement level. However, I found that it was worth the stumble. The window that I tried to raise was indeed unlocked. How did I miss that earlier? Had someone been out there that afternoon? The thought made my stomach queasy but it was offset by feeling relieved that we did not have to puncture the evening's silence by performing a bump and grind on the front door.

I quickly crawled through the window, and found the stairway that led me back to the main level and the front door. I let Greg in and was grateful that the moon was full so that we did not have to turn on any lights. Once my eyes adjusted to the dark, I led Greg into the living room, which was combined with the dining room. I estimated that it was about twenty-eight feet long. Yes, twenty-eight running feet of uninterrupted chocolate-brown, short-shag carpet.

We each picked a corner and began to pull. Greg struggled getting started so I stopped and crossed the room to help him. Once that was done, we both yanked the carpet up from the wooden strips around the perimeter of the room. Then on our hands and knees we began to roll. It was a pretty strenuous workout for a couple of mama's boys. Still, we could "butch it up" when needed, especially knowing the reward would be new carpet.

"Holy moly. I think I am going to have a heart attack," Greg said breathlessly.

"Me, too. Now man up and help me move this sucker out the door," I responded.

If anyone could have seen the pair of us as we struggled to drag, lift and kick that big-ass roll of carpet into my car, they would have been in hysterics. However, I did feel as if I was going to pass out from the exertion – something that I will freely admit that I had not experienced in a very long time. Finally, when we had the carpet loaded, I carefully steered my car down the winding drive and headed across town toward our home with my trunk lid open wide and our evening's reward in full view.

It was after midnight when I backed my car into the parking space in front of our apartment. Fortunately, we had only fifteen feet from my trunk, across the sidewalk and through our front door. We tried our best to be as quiet as possible, since we had neighbors' apartments lined up in rows down each side and across the parking lot. We did not want to attract anyone's curiosity as to why a roll of carpet was being dragged in the wee hours of the morning especially since, according to some movies and TV shows, this is a popular way to dispose of a body!

Finally, everything was inside the apartment and the trunk lid closed. I stood there wondering how on earth this carpet was going to magically be installed but then decided I had reached the point of being too tired to care.

"So now what?" Greg eagerly asked me.

Oh my God... did he actually think that I was going to start installing carpet right then and there? If so, girlfriend was sadly mistaken. I desperately needed my beauty rest.

"Bed is now what. I have got to get some rest. We both have work tomorrow," I answered. Of course, mine was the morning shift while Greg worked the late afternoon shift.

"Go to bed. Dream in chocolate," I said.

—•—

The next morning I felt as if I had been run over by an 18-wheeler, and the driver had thrown it in reverse and backed up just to make sure he crushed me. Wrestling with that carpet had left me with aches and pains in my arms, legs and my unmentionables. What the hell had I been thinking? Or had I finally just lost my mind? And yet, as I came down the steps and saw that mouth-watering roll of shagginess waiting for me, I decided that it was worth it knowing just how good it would look once it was laid. *(Laid? Jeez, laid was something that roll of carpet and I both desperately needed!)*

Anyway, Greg and I had Sunday off — which was only two days away. Our work schedules rarely put us home at the same time. And since it would take both of us to move furniture out of the way just to unroll the carpet, I convinced him that we needed to wait.

I had recently tackled hanging wallpaper — how hard could it be to install carpet? I was about to find out.

Sunday morning came and the first thing that we did was move everything out of the living room and into our kitchen and dining area. Then, once again on our hands and knees, we unrolled our treasure on top of our existing carpet, which I had decided to use as additional padding. The roll of chocolate-brown, short-shag delight was pretty much the same width as our room but much longer.

With our sharpest kitchen knife, I raggedly cut off the extra length to use on the stairs. Once everything was trimmed as close as I could manage, I began hammering the tacks through two layers of carpet and into the existing carpet strips. I was concerned about the noise and our next-door neighbors. We had never formally met them but shared a common wall. However, I kept on working until I had the living room looking good. We moved the furniture back into place and the few flaws visible from my lack of carpet-laying skills were successfully camouflaged. I was grateful to Greg for staying out of my way until I asked for his help. He was like a kid on Christmas morning – so excited with his present.

The stairs would be the next thing to tackle but they were positioned on the opposite common wall shared with neighbors we did know. A pair of fun but very nosy queens, Jim and Jack. It would be hard enough to explain why we were blessed with new carpet, but even more difficult if they realized that we were installing it ourselves in an apartment we did not own. I told Greg that we needed to wait until we were sure that they were not home before nailing the carpet on the steps.

It was midmorning and I felt confident that Jim and Jack were barely out of bed. Patience is not one of my virtues so I convinced Greg that we should go out before the church crowd and have an early lunch. Hopefully our neighbors would be gone by the time we got home. It was a good plan in theory, and yes, they were actually gone when we got back home and started working. However, before I finished, they had returned and neither Greg nor I had realized that. Bang, bang, bang as I hammered nail after nail into the wooden steps. It felt as if the sound rumbled through the entire apartment complex. And then I heard additional banging and realized it was someone knocking on our front door.

"Crap," was all that I could say as I looked at Greg and shrugged. I cracked the door open and there were Jim and Jack.

"Hey there... so what's new?" said Jim, the more full-figured of the two. "Are you going to let us in?"

"Gurrrlll, when did you get new carpet?" Jim continued before I opened the door wider.

I went into full thespian mode and said it was a remnant leftover from a job, which I got for a steal. Yes, I remember I actually said "a steal." And then I went on to tell them that we could not afford to hire someone to install it so we were doing it ourselves. Fortunately, the living room looked presentable but I was already making a mess with my effort on the stairs. Regardless, they seemed to buy what I was selling and clearly were a tad jealous, which certainly sweetened the deal for me.

"Leftover from a job? What job?" asked Jack, the more attractive of the two men.

Oops, details, he wants details. I broke out the old "friend of a friend" excuse, which seemed to appease him for a bit. Neither Jim nor Jack would qualify as rocket scientists but they did have a fair amount of common sense. And Jack at least had the cuteness factor going for him especially when, like now; he was in his very short cutoff blue jeans and no underwear. I was not willing to go anywhere near the truth with them regarding our latest achievement.

I opened the door wider and the boys came in and dropped down on the sofa. I did not want an audience while I continued to butcher the stairs so I decided to take a break and join them. We gossiped for a bit and then they went home with me apologizing in advance for the noise I planned on making as I finished hammering the new carpet into place.

Finally, it was done and if you did not look too closely, it looked pretty good. I pitied the apartment management when the time came for us to move out and they tried to pull up the hundreds of nails that I had used to secure the new carpet.

Our two-bedroom town house now had new kitchen wallpaper and draperies. It also had new chocolate-brown, short-shag carpet in the living room and stairway and an antiqued gold umbrella stand and lovely new side chair. I knew that this was just the beginning.

—●—

Later Jim, Jack and I did decide to play a practical joke on Greg. You see, one night in their apartment, Greg got a bit tipsy and sat on the wall-hung sink in their powder room. The sink immediately went crashing to the floor with his ass sitting in the sink bowl and water spraying everywhere. Since all of us had a buzz from a few cocktails of our own, everyone broke out into hysterical laughter. If it had happened in this decade, someone would have pulled out their phone and snapped a picture. But unfortunately, that was not the case in the 1970s. Still that image will always be etched into my brain.

Jim and Jack had been waiting to get back at Greg ever since that night and so a plan was hatched. While Greg was at work one evening, the three of us painted his bedroom cotton-candy, Pepto-Bismol pink. And as soon as everything was dry, we put his furniture and art back into place and waited.

Greg came in from work late that night and went straight to his room. He knew something was different but everything was in its place. Still, it looked pink and his first thought was that I had replaced the standard light bulb in his swag lamp with a pink bulb. But then it began to sink in that it wasn't the light... the walls had actually been painted pink! Of course, the joke was on us. Instead of being horrified, he was thrilled. Loved it!

For as long as I continued to live there, I had to see the pink glow from across the hall. However as it turned out, I did not live there that much longer.

Chapter Five

I met someone. Well, actually Greg introduced us. But still, someone who liked me – really liked me and who wanted me to move in with him. How can you argue with true love? Oh, if only I had.

I decided that I wanted to be with him and live with him, even though I hated his house, his family and his job. Still he wanted me and whether it was lust or love, I told Greg that I had to give it a try. I knew that Greg was disappointed but in no time at all, he had found another roommate. He ended up regretting his decision every bit as much as I came to regret mine.

Bill was an inch or so taller than me with straight brown hair. I thought he was very handsome. He was soft-spoken, rather low key and more importantly, appeared to be crazy about me. One downside for me was his job. He was a restaurant manager and worked morning, noon and night at the same motel where Greg managed the front desk. Another downside for me was that instead of finding a place of our own, I moved into his home. I use that term lightly because as it turned out, his home was anything but *his*. It was financed by his dad, who lived out of state and guess what? He loved to visit, and of course, he stayed with us in spite of the fact that he was clearly not fond of me. Needless to say, I was equally less than thrilled at sharing the house with anyone's father, especially Bill's.

Bill worked long hours and seven days a week, which gave me lots of quality time with his dad. I would look for excuses to stay away until I felt sure that Bill was off work and headed home. It was my last semester of college, so I needed, and chose, to spend a great deal of time on campus. Finally I graduated college with plans to conquer the world before it conquered me.

I did enjoy living with Bill when his dad would go back to where he belonged. It gave me the chance to see that maybe a romantic relationship could work. But as soon as I got into the groove, his dad would be back on our, I mean, his doorstep to check on things.

Did I put my thieving ways on hold, especially since Bill did not know about my past? Well, that would be a big fat "No." Bill would talk about wanting to fix up his home and I wanted to make him happy. I continued to use my spare time circling construction sites, checking out the possibilities.

I did enjoy *borrowing* a light fixture or two on occasion, and without any electrical skills, I was known to shock myself sometimes as I tried to remove it from the ceiling. I knew I needed to turn the power off but I would get in a hurry and a mistake would happen. After a couple of shocking experiences, I got into the habit of simply yanking it from the ceiling as quickly as I could, instead of carefully unscrewing and disengaging it properly.

One of my funnier chandelier stories happened during my time with Bill. I knew my paramour yearned for a matching pair of colonial brass chandeliers in the oversized room where we shared a bed. The style was fairly common in new construction and I found just what I had been looking for – and I stashed it in the trunk of my car. I thought that I remembered seeing an identical one in another new home and ran by there, yanked it from the ceiling and also placed it in my trunk. However, upon closer inspection, I realized that one chandelier was a 6-light model and the other was a 5-light version. I was thoroughly aggravated, slammed the trunk and began an exhaustive search for a match. Several hours later, I found another 5-light fixture, which caused me to grab the 6-light original find and toss it to the side of the road. That's right, I just tossed it to the side of the road.

Bill was thrilled with his pair of gifts and I was grateful that he knew better than to question me about their origins. However, he did mention a couple of other things that he wondered if I might be able to "find." And with a knowing smile, he offered to lend his assistance in helping me to procure them.

The gig was up!

Bill wanted in!

My thieving partnership with Greg was about to grow into a threesome.

—•—

"What do you mean you told him? Are you crazy? I thought the code was that we told no one the truth," Greg ranted nonstop after I shared with him what had happened. "How could you be so stupid?"

I really could not argue with him. I had brought Greg into the thieving business and had made him promise that he would never tell anyone. No one could be trusted other than ourselves. That was our code and I just broke it for a love that was already flashing warning signs because of Bill's visiting father.

"I know. You are right. I messed up," I pleaded with him. At the same time I thought, you better enjoy this because I will not be apologizing again. I had reached my limit. Inside my head I am screaming *shut the hell up. Yes, I messed up. Yes, Greg chastised me. But now, I am done. It was time to move on and I knew just what it would take to get Greg's mind off of my blunder. Another midnight run.*

"Are you done?" I said with as much restraint as I could muster. Greg opened his mouth but I stopped him right there.

"It was a rhetorical question. You seem to be a tad confused so let me make this clear. You are done," I said with purpose. Greg knew that tone well enough to close his mouth. "Now, may I interest you in a job?"

"What? Seriously?" he stammered. "You better not be messing with me." Greg's eyes lit up and his mouth began to water.

I wanted to ask "Or what?" but then decided we needed to move on and I needed him in a better mood.

I had found a place nearby with five furnished models. They were not furnished by one of our local stores but by a designer out of state. I had walked through the models during the past Sunday's open house along with so many other potential buyers that I felt confident that I was not even noticed. In situations like that, I make an effort to blend in by not asking questions or starting conversations.

At this point you may be wondering why we would be taking huge risks to steal furniture. Unlike today's massed-produced, assemble-yourself-imports, furniture in the 1970s and 1980s was mostly made in America. It was heavy, solid wood in beautiful rich finishes. Furniture stores would have deliverymen in trucks bring it to you and set it up in your home. It was not inexpensive, flimsy and poorly crafted. It was not something that you would toss out once you were tired of it or something that would fall apart in a very short period of time. People would dip into their savings or work out a financing plan just to be able purchase pieces, which they hoped to hand down to their children. And as guys in our twenties, with low-income jobs, stealing was the perfect solution for us to acquire these luxuries.

"When?" Greg asked.

"Well, if you promise to be good, maybe tonight," I replied. I then went on to explain the downside.

"The condos have basement garages, so there is no way to go in through the back and no windows on the lower level to leave unlocked. Plus the front windows on the main level are the difficult crank-out kind, which I loathe. So the only way in would be to break down the front door. However, once we are in, we can go downstairs and open the garage door and even pull the car inside to load. But busting through the front door is the most risky part. Also, there is no way in hell that we can do five models in one night and naturally, once it has been discovered, we will not be able to go back," I said.

"Say no more. I'm ready," said Greg excitedly.

"There were two models that I thought had the most desirable furnishings." I continued, ignoring Greg's interruption. "You will have to just trust me on this. We will break into one, do our damage and if it still looks safe, then maybe a second model. But that's all. It would be nuts for us to get so greedy that we might get caught."

I could tell that Greg wasn't 100% on board with hitting just a couple of models when five were available, but he knew better than to question me. I had kept us both safe so far and hoped that he trusted me to not put us at a greater risk than necessary.

The anticipation of knowing something risky was about to happen but having to wait made us both a little crazy. Neither one of us had much of an appetite for dinner. And not to be too graphic, but when I get nervous my digestive system goes haywire.

"Your stomach upset?" Greg asked with sincere concern.

"You reading my mind?" I answered nauseously.

"No, your face – it looks a bit green. And honestly, I think it is catching. I am a little queasy too," Greg answered.

With that, we both decided it would not be the dumbest thing if we each put a few napkins or Kleenex in our pockets, just in case. Furnished models don't always provide the bathroom essentials. In fact, I have even seen where they have tied a ribbon around the toilet seat to keep people from using it. Seriously, they gift-wrapped the crapper!

"It's ten," Greg said.

"I know. Just thinking it over in my mind. This one is riskier than the others," I added.

I had decided that we would go in my car and if everything worked out well with the first load, then maybe – just maybe – I would let Greg bring his car on the second load. I had not shared that with him yet because I was not sure that it was the smartest move. Still, it was an option but an even bigger gamble.

I pulled into the complex around 10:45 and made one pass down the main drive. The models were all attached so I knew no one lived in that row of buildings. It did appear that one row of condos was completed and possibly lived in, but with garages and no interior lights on, I could not be sure if anyone was at home. There was another row of condos that looked to be about halfway finished. I parked my car in a guest spot near the clubhouse that faced a swimming pool.

The night sky was black with very few stars. A few lamps in each model home had been left on and light spilled out through the windows onto the front sidewalk. I was grateful that the exterior lights had been left off so as not to illuminate our arrival. Greg, who was as excited as a drag queen in a women's shoe store, began peering through the windows motioning for me to take a look. I knew that he would not be happy unless we emptied each model but still I shook my head and mouthed "No." I waved for him to come back to one of the units which I felt was most promising from my earlier visit. But just to be sure, I tried each and every front door in hopes that one would have accidentally been left unlocked. However, no such luck.

I pushed on the front door and then bumped it with my shoulder. Nothing. Next I threw my backside into it and felt a bit of movement. Greg gave me a gentle shove and then he tried the same. This was a stubborn door and I kept looking around to make sure I did not see lights come on in the other finished building or anyone out for a stroll. We took turns until it finally gave way with a thundering crack. I yanked Greg inside and closed the door quickly. I told him to hold it shut while I rushed to an upstairs window in a dark bedroom where I could observe. I wanted to be sure that no one was coming to check out the noise. As I patiently watched and waited, I thought to myself that there was no way that I wanted to break into another unit or two if it was going to make that much racket.

I had only been gone for just a few minutes, although it felt much longer. I came back downstairs and we began to gather up the goodies. Since Greg had not been in the model earlier, he ran through room after room to make sure that he saw everything before making his decisions. Once we had a game plan, we began to take things downstairs to the garage, leaving room for me to eventually pull my car inside. Paintings! Yes, this designer used original art, along with small furniture pieces, lamps, accessories, linens and even kitchen items all found their way to the garage.

"This is more than one load. Maybe two or three," Greg said.

"I know," I confirmed. "I think I need to go ahead and move my car."

I went back out the front door and walked down the sidewalk to my Buick sedan. It still looked clear and no lights had come on in the adjoining building. I started the car and moved it around to the back of the unit where Greg had raised the garage door allowing me to pull in. I had already unhooked the electric door so that we could quietly raise and lower it manually. Once the car was inside and the door lowered, we began to load everything in. Although I still wanted to be quick, knowing that we were protected by being inside allowed us to load much more systematically and pack the car carefully. It was surprising just how much the backseat and trunk could hold. And then I loaded Greg into the front seat and filled his lap with carefully packed breakables before opening the garage door.

There was that split second where I pictured police with guns waiting for us once the door opened. But fortunately, it was still dark and silent with no signs of activity as I backed my car out of the garage and lowered the door.

We quickly and quietly unloaded the contents from my car into Greg's living room. Jim and Jack still lived next door and we did not want to alert them. Once that was done, there was no time to enjoy our stash. We needed to hustle if we expected to grab more before sunrise. It was now or never. I had to make a decision and I prayed that it was not the wrong one.

"Why don't you follow me so that we will have two cars?" I said, looking at Greg. It took a few seconds for that to register with him and when it did, a huge smile came across his face. He nodded and went to get into his 1971 Ford Maverick.

Once again, I pulled around back, raised the garage door and pulled my car inside. Greg parked nearby and walked over just as I was ready to pull the door back down.

"How does this work?" he asked.

"Let's finish loading my car. I think everything will fit. Then if it still looks clear, we will tackle another model and you can move your car into that garage," I replied.

We managed to get everything in my car with a bit of room leftover. I suggested that we make one more sweep of the unit and see what we still might fit in. Another small table, a couple of lamps and a few throw pillows got tossed in before I declared it full. With two cars, I now had the passenger side of my front seat available for more items.

Leaving my car in the garage, we walked out the front door and two doors down to the other unit of my choosing. Bump, kick, push, bump again and the door gave way. As before, I ran upstairs and looked out from a dark bedroom to make sure that I did not see any activity outside. And, once again, it appeared to be clear. I suggested to Greg that he move his car immediately so that no one would be aware of anyone being there.

With the garage door unhooked and manually raised, Greg pulled his car inside and I closed the door behind him. This was another of those fearful moments that we were both trapped with our cars in the garages and no way to make a hasty getaway. I told myself to take a deep breath and get busy. But first, grateful for the Kleenex in my pocket, I needed a bathroom.

It was now after one in the morning and we were still running like we had bathed in caffeine. This was a smaller two-bedroom town house but had more things that I thought were special. I think Greg felt the same as we began to gather. A small desk, a huge yellow floral oil painting, a set of dining chairs and the usual tables, lamps accessories and linens. Other than the desk, everything was small enough for one person to handle.

Greg's car was overflowing and still there was more at the bottom of the steps that we planned to take with us. The time had come where we both needed to get in our cars and carefully drive home. I opened the garage door and let Greg back out and pulled the door down again. I walked over to the other unit, opened the door and backed my car out. Once the garage door was down, I led the procession back to Greg's apartment.

As soon as Greg opened his apartment door, we heard the phone ringing. A chill ran down my spine. Would the police call if someone had reported seeing one of our cars and caught our license tag number?

"What do I do?" Greg asked in a panicked tone.

"Answer it, you fool. What choice do we have?" I replied.

Greg went to the kitchen wall phone, picked up the receiver and hesitantly said "Hello."

"It's for you," Greg said with a smirk.

Bill. Of course it would be Bill. I had left a message for him at work that Greg and I were going to a movie and since it would be late, and Greg's roommate had already moved out, I was going to stay the night with him. Naturally Bill did not buy that story for a minute and had been trying to reach me ever since he got off work at midnight. He explained that he had been calling and calling and lo and behold, we were not there.

"Are you okay?" Bill asked. "Where have you been? Or more importantly, have you been careful?"

I felt like he was peering through the phone line and already aware of our evening rendezvous. At least he had the good sense not to ask what movie we had been to. There was no need to lie. He was clearly aware that we had been into some mischief.

"Do you want me to come over?" he asked.

"No, we were just going to bed. I will fill you in tomorrow. And I might have a present or two for you if you promise to be a good boy," I sweetly replied.

I caught Greg rolling his eyes and my hand automatically raised with my middle finger at attention.

"I promise everything is okay but you will just have to wait until tomorrow," I said but, then realized that it was already tomorrow and corrected myself. "I mean, later today. But for now, we all need to get some sleep."

"Are we not going back?" Greg asked once I hung up the phone.

"Of course we are going back. But first we need to unload our cars," I sharply answered.

It was now almost three in the morning, the time when the local bartenders would start yelling "Last call" followed by the house lights coming up, with the harsh reality of seeing behind the curtain and the ugliness of everything and everyone.

Time had run out for breaking down one more door but we still had things ready and waiting in the garage of the second unit. Greg wanted to take his car again but I assured him that we could get everything that was left in my car.

"Then we need to get as far away from that place as quickly as possible," I added.

The complex still looked as deserted as before and there were no signs that anyone had discovered the damage we had done earlier. However, there was that split second flash in my brain that wondered if the cops might have been called, and were waiting inside the garage. I took a deep breath, opened the door, relieved to find no one there and drove inside for the last time.

It did not take long to put the remaining items in my car and even run back upstairs to add a few more. Later, Greg and I both gasped for air when I pulled my car into the parking space in front of Greg's apartment. I don't think either of us had been aware of holding our breath for the last few miles.

"I can't even," Greg moaned.

"Me neither, but we have to get this stuff out of my car," I added.

"I don't think there is any more room left inside," Greg commented with a smile. "But that would not stop me from going back for more."

I noticed that the sky appeared to be getting lighter in anticipation of the coming sunrise as we brought the last of the night's haul inside. We were both anxious to pick and choose but dividing everything would have to come later. I needed sleep before heading into work in a few hours. Reluctantly, we went to bed.

–●–

The alarm went off way too early and I was not sure that I could even get out of bed. Once again, my body was rebelling from the previous night's activities. I thought to myself, I am stiff and sore and every part of me ached. And then my sexual deviant mind went straight to the gutter – *stiff and sore? Hmmm...* I had to laugh.

The excitement of what was waiting downstairs propelled me out of the bed. I slipped my clothes back on and quietly descended the chocolate-brown, short-shag carpeted stairs. I wanted a few minutes to take it all in and make a game plan before Greg got up. I was sure that he already had in mind what pieces that he wanted, as did I. So I needed a moment to figure out what was worth fighting over and what I would be happy to let go of. Knowing Greg, I decided that I could act as if I wanted something afterward which would make him want it too. That way I could focus my attention on something I really did not want and then let Greg talk me out of it – allowing me to choose something that I really did want. Does that make sense?

But first of all, I needed to figure out what Bill might like so that I could appease him and stay in his good graces. Definitely one of the lamps looked promising and a couple of framed prints.

I was concentrating so hard that I did not realize Greg was standing on the stairs watching me.

"So?" asked Greg.

"I have got a little time if you want to go ahead and divide up everything," I offered.

"Sure, sounds good," Greg said, with a terrible poker face as he tried his best to mask his excitement.

"I am sure that you have already got some ideas. I do too. Plus, I need to give Bill a thing or two," I said.

"Why? He wasn't a part of any of this and does not even know where we hit or how much we ended up with," Greg said with a bit of attitude.

He was totally correct. I was only thinking of giving Bill things because we were in this relationship and he suspected something.

"True. I am not saying to divide everything in thirds. We will split it down the middle and I will give him something from my half," I conceded.

"I don't know why, but whatever," Greg said dismissively.

I offered to let Greg choose first. I thought that we could go back and forth taking turns. And then if there was something the other one got and wanted to trade, we could work something out.

"Does that sound fair?" I asked.

"Yes, and I will start with the yellow floral painting," Greg quickly answered.

I was okay with that. I said the desk would be my first selection. Uh oh, the look on Greg's face made me realize that he had wanted it as well. So I offered for him to choose two things next, since the desk was a bigger item.

"Great. I choose this table and that lamp," Greg said.

Damn. That was the lamp I wanted for Bill.

"Okay, then I will take this table," I continued.

"I want that picture," Greg added.

"This lamp," I replied.

"I would like the bedspread," he said.

Back and forth we went until everything was spoken for. We grouped some of the smaller things together so as not to nickel and dime it to death. And finally, all the decisions had been made and I think both of us were fairly pleased.

"Not too shabby for a night's work," Greg concluded.

—●—

I was not in the mood to go to my job but I jumped into the shower, borrowed a shirt from Greg and headed out. All day long I kept thinking about everything we had acquired the night before and wished that I had my own place to fix up and not Bill's father's house. *Did I not want to be in a relationship? I was not sure anymore. I did like him and I liked the idea of having a lover, a partner, but was Bill the one? Would I feel differently if his father was not so much a part of our life together?* Regardless, I had nowhere else to put my treasures. I had no choice but to take my things to his house and hope for the best.

I did not want Bill to know all of the details of the heist and I especially did not want him to know just how much Greg and I had actually stolen. I called Greg from work and explained all of this to him. I still had a key to his place and asked him if it would be okay if I went by after I got off from work and loaded up my car.

Greg was at work by the time I got to his apartment. I let myself in and was surprised that Greg had already placed most of his pieces. Without a roommate, he had some empty spots to fill and several of the pieces went into the spare bedroom. I loaded up my car and was grateful not to see any neighbors in the process. I did not take everything, so as not to overwhelm Bill, and left a few things in the closet in Greg's spare room.

I was grateful that Bill was at work and that his father was back at his out-of-state home so that I could take my time unloading and arranging everything. I hung a few pictures and moved some things of Bill's to make room for the new table and another lamp that I had planned on being his. I felt that was a generous gift for someone who had not found, planned or executed the theft.

I was exhausted from the night before and struggled to stay awake until Bill got home. Fortunately, it was one of his earlier nights. He called before leaving the restaurant to give me a head's up, saying he was on his way and excited. *Excited?* Something told me the only excitement he was feeling was for what he was anxious to find when he got home in the form of material possessions and not me. And I was correct.

He did love my gift of the square table with slate top, plus the Oriental vase lamp and several small accessories. And he was happy that I had added a few other pieces to our decor. He wanted to know the details of our night but all that I shared with him was my carefully constructed story. I downplayed the volume of items that were available and played up the risk in hopes of discouraging him from wanting to go back out there. But then he wanted to know what Greg got and if it would be something he would rather have than what I had brought home.

Wait a second... warning sirens were going off in my head. All of a sudden Bill had an opinion and thought that he had a say in what we got and how we divided it? *Hell no.*

I did my best to not say what I was thinking but I am pretty sure that he saw the look in my eyes and realized that he had gone too far. He then quickly changed his tune and said how appreciative he was of everything and the risk that we took to have these beautiful pieces in our home. *Good boy. Smart move.*

"Is there more? I mean do you want to go back and see what else we could get?" Bill asked.

Oh Bill, you should have stopped while you were ahead.

Chapter Six

"*I am ready. Put me in*, coach," Bill said a few days later.

"Seriously? I know you did not just use sports terminology on me," I said in disbelief. "I mean, I may have been the school mascot but my knowledge of sports can be summed up in three words. Balls and tight end."

"I am serious. I want to go on a 'midnight run.' Isn't that what you are calling it? It wouldn't be my first time," Bill said as he tried to not laugh at my comment.

"Okay, now you have my attention. What did you mean by that?" I asked.

He proceeded to explain that he had stolen before as he pointed to several of the architectural elements in his home.

"That mantel came from an old house downtown and the stained glass window from an abandoned church out on 5th," he said.

"What else?" I asked now that he had my attention.

"Well, that statue by the patio came from the city cemetery and the iron piece by the front door from a railing of a home about to be torn down a little ways west of town," Bill continued.

I could see him puff up a bit. He was proud of his accomplishments.

"Okay, but those really do not compare to breaking and entering. I mean those pieces came from places that were deserted, about to be torn down and such. Of course, there may be some relatives upset about the statue missing from their loved one's grave. But still, I am not sure it is in the same league," I said.

"I disagree. It may not be like your fancy new furniture but I still took risks and could have easily been arrested for what I did. Regardless, I think that I am qualified to help you. I mean I can do everything Greg can do. And even replace him, if you wanted me to," Bill said testily.

"Let me make this clear, there is no replacing Greg. He is not only my best friend but let's face it, look at the crap he has on me. I would not want to piss him off. Fine, let me see what I can find and then we will figure out a plan," I said as I tried to keep from sounding angry.

I realized that I needed to tread carefully. I had to keep Bill and Greg happy and not make them feel as if they were competing with each other. I certainly did not need anyone getting so upset that they felt threatened or revengeful. I needed my boys to stay happy.

—•—

Bill and Greg were in the same situation in that they both worked night shifts and I worked days. But Bill's schedule could sometimes tie him up during the daytime as well. Still, that left my late afternoons free to go exploring on my own and now that summer was here and the days were longer, I had a little over two hours of daylight left to investigate after work.

Other condominium projects were popping up around town but I was not totally sure that I wanted to start Bill with something that large. I also was not completely sure that I could rein him in like Greg, especially if he got in his mind that more is not enough. I was sure that Bill would have wanted to break in all five of those model units from the last job no matter the risk. No, I needed something relatively small and easy to start with just so I could get a feeling how he would do under pressure.

"I think that I have found something that you would like," I said one afternoon.

Bill sat upright anxiously waiting for more details.

"It is a rug, and not just any rug but a custom plush wool area rug. It is large and the only room that it would fit in would be the one your dad stays in when he's here," I managed to say without gritting my teeth. "It may be a bit feminine but it is beautiful. And I am familiar with the New York company that made it and I would imagine that it is worth several thousand dollars."

It was in a large Georgian-style home currently on the market in the old money part of town. I had stopped by and looked through the windows earlier and although the homeowners had moved out, the rug remained. I thought that the rug was custom designed and probably purchased for that particular room. I assumed that either it would not fit in their new place or that the realtor had suggested leaving it as a perk for marketing the home.

It seemed that any house coming on the market in the wealthy area of town was vacant. I think that the homeowners simply felt that they would not want the riffraff checking out their furnishings during an open house. Plus, they could probably afford to move out and have two mortgages. Who am I kidding? I doubt that they even had one mortgage. Anyway, the house was vacant and a key had been hidden.

In the 1970s, realtors often hid keys and I had the knack for being able to find them. Over the door was a popular spot, or under a planter or doormat. However, in this case, I noticed a rock that seemed out of place sitting in the landscaping by the front door. When I turned it over, I found a key partially hidden in the dirt and thought to myself "Bingo."

Let me share this little tidbit with you from my past experiences... sometimes the key does not work on the door that it is placed next to. The first time that this happened to me, I thought: *What the hell?* I wondered why a key was left outside that did not work on the door. But then, on a lark, I took the key around to a side door and voilà, it worked. That actually happened to me three times now. Some poor fool thought that they were being so clever.

I let myself in and relocked the door, not wanting anyone to slip in and surprise me. I made a quick sweep of the house and unlocked a side window, just in case I wanted to come back later and found that the key was gone. The home was elegant, just as you would expect. High ceilings, beautiful wallpaper, dark-stained oak floors except for the black and white marble floor in the powder room. The wall sconces in that bath were gold leaf and had little silk shades covering the bulbs. I thought that I would not mind too much having the pair for myself. However, over the vanity, only a hook remained where I felt sure an antique mirror had hung.

I continued down the hall and saw a walnut paneled library lined with shelves and a black marble fireplace. I noticed there was not a ceiling light fixture, only a junction box. So often in the richy-rich homes, people exclude from the sale their chandeliers and take them to their next home. The kitchen, however, was disappointing. It had clearly not been remodeled in a very long time. The appliances were dated but at least were quality brands. Adjoining the kitchen was a garden room, where perfectly centered in the room, lay a custom wool rug in ivory with borders of leaves in pink and green. It was in pristine condition and was either new or that room never had much traffic – and definitely no pets.

I rushed back to my car and grabbed my tape measure because I liked to be prepared. I quickly measured the rug from side to side and realized that there was only one room in our home where it would fit – his father's room. What an absolute waste of an elegant rug, having Bill's dad's fuzzy bedroom slippers walking on it. And I am sure that he would have lots to say about a rug in pink and green in "his" bedroom. Still, he would not be around forever (hopefully) and regardless, the rug was too fabulous not to come home with me. Or I should say, the home I shared with Bill?

"So, a rug and a pair of sconces? That's it?" Bill asked in a disappointed tone.

"What? You were expecting more?" I was trying to not raise my voice. "If you don't think it's worth your time, then I will let Greg know and see if he would want to help me." That was all it took.

"No, no, I want it. Thank you. What is your plan?" Bill said with an immediate change of attitude.

Some jobs work better at night and, others during the middle of the day. To me, this was a day job. That area of town had its own police force that patrolled regularly, especially at night.

"I actually have Friday off this week. If you can tear yourself away from the lunch crowd, I'd say let's shoot for then," I said. That was two days away and I hoped that the key would still be there or at least the window might still be unlocked. I had unlocked windows only to return later and found some observant busybody must have noticed and locked them back.

Bill drove a 1973 Oldsmobile Vista Cruiser station wagon, so I suggested that we take his car as it would be easier to load, and he agreed.

"You're not telling Greg, are you?" Bill added.

"No, this will just be us," I said, already feeling guilty about not including Greg. He would have loved the rug too, but then I rationalized that he did not have a room large enough in his apartment to accommodate it. Still, it felt like that I was cheating on him.

— ● —

Friday came and Bill had to run by the restaurant but promised that he would not stay long. I had yet to say anything to Greg and preferred not saying anything at all or at least waiting until it was a done deal. I was beginning to pace when Bill returned around 11:30. He was anxious and in a hurry because they were short-staffed that day and he really needed to be at work.

"Do you want to wait until another day? Or even later today?" I asked.

"No, let's do it, but we need to be quick," Bill answered.

"Really, we can go now or after your lunch crowd thins out. It does not matter. I don't want you going if you are too stressed," I offered.

He first said that he was fine, but then thought for a moment before he asked if I was sure it would be okay if we waited a couple of hours. To be truthful, I was relieved because one, he was dry-humping my last gay nerve and two, I did not need him being careless because he felt rushed.

"Yes, please go back. I have got things that I can do and we will just plan on going later," I said, feeling slightly relieved.

I really did not have anything to do but wait, which tends to make me antsy. However, I felt better about going later when the time was right and not forcing the situation when Bill was already agitated.

Finally, he got home around three, nervous at what we were about to do. But at least he was no longer worried about the restaurant. Good. I needed him focused. Even though we were taking his car, I said that I would drive. The home was on my former side of town so I was familiar with the ins and outs of the neighborhood. He did not put up any resistance and dutifully rode shotgun.

Bill was blown away by the house when I pulled into the drive. And rightfully so. We could only dream about having a home like that. I told him that even though we can't afford to live there, we could at least own a little piece of it. I pulled his car around to the side garage where a thicket of trees and shrubs offered a screen between the house and its neighbor. I told Bill to wait as I jumped out and ran around to find the key. Fortunately, it was still there and I was able to let myself in, relock the door and run to let Bill in through the side door. He began walking through the house, talking about this and that.

"Bill, get a grip," I said snapping him back to reality. "We are not moving in but we are moving things out and we need to get on with it." I led him into the garden room and his first view of the rug. He quickly saw it was every bit as spectacular as I had described and turned to me and smiled. Okay, my heart melted. Then I led him to the powder room and showed him the sconces. He agreed that we needed them.

"Uh oh, I need to go to the bathroom. All of a sudden, my stomach is upset," Bill said in desperation. He was so relieved that they had left toilet paper.

"No need to explain, it happens to me too," I said as I tried to not laugh.

Once he was done, he took the sconces down. I was grateful that I did not have to do it since I would have shocked myself in the process. Bill placed the sconces carefully in his car, being very protective of their silk shades. We then rolled the rug, along with the pad, and dragged it to the door. We each grabbed an end and struggled as we hoisted it through the door and into his car. I swear that it was every bit as heavy as the chocolate-brown, short-shag number that Greg and I had tackled a few months earlier. I started to comment on that but caught myself as I remembered Bill did not know anything about that episode.

The rug was now in the back of the car. We had to leave the rear window down so a part of the rug could hang out. It was time to pull out of the drive and pray that the neighborhood police were not making a pass down the street. I had been caught speeding by them before, so I was very careful to stay within the speed limit.

We made it home safely and then emptied the extra bedroom of all of its furnishings so that we could put the new rug in place. Wow! Simply wow! It looked so good. In fact, it looked better than some of the furniture pieces that were going back into the room. I thought to myself: we might need to be upgrading them soon.

—●—

"Are you sitting down?" Bill asked when I picked up the phone. It was now several days after our shopping spree for a custom rug and wall sconces in the highfalutin area of town.

He was calling from work and I never like a conversation to start that way. My mind immediately goes to the police tracking us down.

"What is it, Bill?" I hesitantly asked.

"My father is coming for a visit next week," he replied.

Bloody hell.

"Wasn't he just here, or am I imagining that?" I continued.

"He was here last month but this time it's different," he answered with reserve.

"Different how?" I asked feeling my stomach starting to get tied up in knots.

"My sister is coming, too. They both are staying with us," Bill blurted out quickly.

Profanities were on the edge of my tongue. I had only met his sister once and she, like his father, did not approve of me. At that time she asked Bill, with me standing there, why he needed a roommate. Followed by wanting to know if he could not afford to live on his own.

"Both of them in our home? For, for, for how long, Bill?" I stuttered.

"Probably a couple of weeks, or at least my dad will be here that long," he answered.

"I am going to ask Greg if I can stay with him. There is no way that your father, sister and I can live under one roof with you always at work," I said adamantly.

"Don't be silly, they like you. It will be fine," Bill said trying to reassure me.

"First of all, no, they hate me. And no, it will not be fine. We need a place of our own and let your dad have this one," I said firmly.

"You are overreacting," Bill said accusingly.

I practically bit my tongue but thought: *this isn't being productive and I should wait until we were face to face to continue this discussion.* However, I did have one more question.

"Where is everyone sleeping?" I asked.

The house had three bedrooms. Well, really just two. But Bill had decided that the converted garage would be our room and my Italian provincial bedroom suite would go in one of the smaller bedrooms, while the other room would be for his dad's visits.

What I have not shared with you is that Bill had still not come out to his family. So each two-week visit from his dad had Bill and me sleeping in separate rooms.

"If it's okay with you, my sister could take your room, dad would be in *his* room and then you and I could share the big room," he answered hopefully.

Okay, I did not see that coming. That was definitely a positive in a very negative situation.

"You don't think they will balk at that idea? After all, they think that I am the devil incarnate out to ruin you," I said with as much humor as I could muster under the circumstances.

"They may think that but they don't know it for a fact. Anyway, you are the devil and I am more than willing to let you try and ruin me!" Bill said playfully.

Now he was turning on that charm that made me think anything was possible.

"Fine, I am sure that I can adapt," I relented.

—•—

Bill's father and sister arrived – and guess which one of us had to meet them and which one was at work. That's right, I played the role of gracious host. The three of us were cordial in a cool sort of way. Bill had already explained in advance the sleeping arrangements to them by phone. I helped each by putting their luggage in their bedrooms.

Immediately his father commented about the new rug in his room. Even he could tell it was custom and expensive and wanted to know why it was there.

Bill and I had already rehearsed our stories. Yep, the old "friend of a friend" and "a deal to good to pass up" along with "we both chipped in to afford it." I thought that we were done discussing it but I was wrong. Bill left work early to be there for a late supper and that is when everything hit the fan.

"How can you afford a rug like that? I mean, you couldn't afford this house without my help," said Bill's father.

Yikes, he was going for the jugular right from the start. I could tell Bill was not happy with the direction this was headed.

"Did you buy it to impress Ricky? Did he talk you into it?" Bill's sister chimed in.

I bit my tongue and thought: *Hey bitch, I am sitting right here.*

"And where did that table come from? Or that lamp? Dad said it wasn't here the last time he visited," she added.

"Where are you getting all of this money?" his father butted in.

Bill was stammering, trying to respond, but they were like a tag team of evil out to destroy him and everyone in their way.

"I work hard and long hours with overtime so that I can afford nice things. And Ricky helps with rent," Bill explained.

"Rent? I've never seen any rent. I thought he was just a freeloader," said Daddy Dearest. "I have wondered what he had on you for you to put up with him."

What the hell?

"Freeloader? Surely you did not just call me a freeloader?" I said raising my voice. "I pay my way and help your son as much as you do. That's what couples do for each other."

Oh, crap, I did not just say that.

Bill turned white as a sheet and his father and sister looked at Bill, then me, then back at Bill. I could tell that they were gathering their ammunition and I had a target painted on my forehead.

"I told you he was queer," his sister said looking at their dad.

"I'm not gay," yelled Bill. Causing me to snap my head towards him.

"Not you," she continued. "I didn't say that you're queer. It's him. Ricky." As she pointed her finger at me. "I could tell from the first minute I laid eyes on him that he was funny, odd, peculiar. He's a homo and he's trying to convert you."

"You have got to be kidding me?" I said in disbelief. I stood and said, "I am going because clearly you all have some things to sort out."

I looked at Bill and he looked wounded. He had just been outed by his lover. But I could also see that I had hurt him, which left him confused, conflicted and lost.

"I will be at Greg's," I said and then I grabbed some of my clothes and left.

—•—

"You did what?" Greg asked in disbelief.

"I outed him by accident to his father and sister," I replied.

"Good for you," Greg said gleefully.

"No. It's not good. And I think Bill and I might be done. I can't imagine that he would want anything to do with me after my performance tonight. But those people are horrible. I just couldn't help myself," I said.

"You know that you can stay here as long as you need to," Greg sweetly offered.

"Thanks," I said, as tears ran down my face.

I did not get much sleep that night. I am pretty sure that it was even worse for Bill. Like a coward I ran, but I thought it was for the best. There is no way that my staying there could have helped the situation.

I imagined Bill felt that I had betrayed him and yet, I couldn't help but feel betrayed, too. The man who had professed his love for me did not defend me – did not fight for me.

I tried calling Bill the next day at work, but was told that he was busy and could not come to the phone. I tried again that night at home and there was no answer. I wanted to run by there – after all, it was my home too. But then I thought maybe he just needed some space. However, after two days, I was out of clean clothes and needed to do something. I decided to swing by the restaurant and see if he would talk with me.

I saw him from across the dining room when I walked in. He looked up, gave a half smile and walked over.

"What are you doing here?" he asked.

"I wanted to see you – to know that you are okay. Are you?" I asked with concern.

He motioned for me to follow him outside and I did. He told me that his father and sister had left the next day and that he never confirmed for them that we were a couple. That disappointed me but I had to let Bill deal with things in whatever way was best for him. I asked if I could come back home, or least get some of my clothes and things.

"Come back. We really need to talk and figure some things out. I will be home about nine," he said.

"Thank you. I will be there," I said with a premature feeling of relief.

True to his word, Bill got home around nine. I had made myself nauseous worrying about what he might say, as well as trying to figure out just how I felt about him. I really loved him but there was no way that I could deal with his family. Especially if he could not be honest with them.

We both laid our cards on the table but ultimately; we both knew that it could not continue as it had been. I offered to move out but he was not asking for that. Still, I told him that I could not handle another visit from his family. He agreed and said he was not sure that he could either. His father was very opinionated, as parents can be, but even more so when it involves their money. We agreed to not make any rash decisions and maybe just start over.

I knew that it was not just Bill's family who felt homosexuality was wrong. It was the 1970s and gays and lesbians still had to be careful. At a gay bar or a party in the home of friends, we could be ourselves. But many felt that they could not be out at work for fear of losing their jobs. My own parents, accepting as they were, tried to hide their disappointment at the thought of never having grandchildren. I realized that Bill's family felt being gay was a sin. He had no way of knowing if they would be accepting of his lifestyle or turn against him as the parents of several of our friends had done.

— ● —

For the next week or so, we played house and everything seemed okay with a few reservations. Maybe I was trying to buy love or just make up for my huge blunder, but I ran across a stunning breakfront in another house on the market and knew Bill would love it. It was the only piece of furniture left in the house, which seemed curious. I told Bill about it and for the first time since that eventful night, he looked happy. The house was in a good area of town and yes, a key was hidden over the door.

We once again brought his station wagon and parked it on the circle drive in front of the house during the middle of the day. The breakfront was in two pieces, a base credenza and an upper display piece with glass doors. It was either going to have to be two trips or one piece would need to be strapped to the roof. As it turned out, strapping the glass door upper cabinet to the roof was our only option because it was too wide to fit inside his car. I joked that if we kept this up, we might have to invest in a truck or van.

Bill was prepared with straps to tie it down. He had transported things on his roof before. Everything went like clockwork as we brought the breakfront back to our home – although it didn't really feel like my home anymore. Still, Bill was pleased with the new addition and it did look wonderful in the dining room. We moved the existing buffet into the entrance hall, where I placed the lamp that I had given him along a few accessories displayed on top.

After a couple of months, and no mention of his family, Bill told me that his father wanted to come visit.

"He thinks that you have moved out," Bill added.

"Did you tell him that?" I asked.

"No, he just assumed that you did and I wasn't in the mood to tell him differently. I wish my mother were still alive. She could always talk some sense in him," Bill said longingly.

"Do you want me to move out?" I asked hesitantly.

"No. But it might be best. I don't want to break up. I just think we should try living apart for a while. What do you think?" Bill gently asked.

What I thought was that he had just suckered-punched me in the gut. He was still living a lie and I was about to be the next casualty.

I saw his lips moving, but all I heard was that he wanted me gone.

Chapter Seven

"*Jim and Jack invited us* over for dinner," Greg said with trepidation.

I knew that he was trying to cheer me up and I did need a distraction. I had decided to move back into the same apartment complex that I had left months earlier but told Greg that I would get my own place. He had pretty much filled his apartment and I had added a bunch of new things myself since the last time we had lived together. I rented a one-bedroom unit across the parking lot from the apartment that I had shared with Greg.

"Sounds good. I haven't seen them in a while," I answered and could visibly see Greg's features relax with my reply.

We walked next door to Jim and Jack's apartment. It was good to see them and catch up on the latest drama. We opened the bottle of wine we'd brought and they had some cheese and crackers to munch on before dinner was ready. Jim and Jack had decided to grill out and the hamburgers smelled great. It felt good to just sit and laugh. Greg had enlightened them on my situation and they had welcomed me back to the neighborhood with open arms.

"There is something that we want to talk about with both of you. We have been waiting for just the right time," said the adorable Jack. He was once again in his blue jean cutoffs, which I would have sworn had gotten even shorter, now causing him to partially spill out when he sat down.

"What's up?" I asked.

"Not sure where to start, so I'll just dive in. We want a new dining table and chairs," said Jim.

"Okay. Great," I replied, not knowing where the conversation was headed.

"And we want you to get it for us," Jim continued.

"Huh? What?" said Greg after taking a big bite of his hamburger.

"Let's be frank. We have watched you several times bringing things in during the middle of the night. It has been a while but seriously – carpet, then chairs, tables, lamps and art. You thought that you were being so quiet but I am surprised that everyone in this block didn't hear you," Jim continued now that he was on a roll.

I looked at Greg and he looked at me.

"We were upstairs watching you from our window in the dark," Jim added.

I realized that it was the exact same thing that I done on one of our jobs after we loudly broke down a door just to make sure I did not see anyone coming.

"Don't try and deny it. We know what we saw and we have a pretty good idea of how much you both make at work, so don't try to come up another one of your stories of how some "friend of a friend" gave you this great deal. Tell me that we're wrong," said Jim.

"I can't," I replied, looking him directly in the eyes.

"That's what I thought. Now, we are not being greedy. But we think you might want to find us a dining set as a thank you for staying quiet," Jim proposed.

Did Jim really just say that? Is he blackmailing us? All of a sudden the hamburger did not taste all that good.

"We are not blackmailing you," said Jack, as if he were reading my mind. "It's just that we really want this and can't afford it right now and we thought you might want to help us."

"And," Jim added looking right through me. "That is not the only thing I have noticed. I see how you look at Jack – always trying to catch a glimpse when he crosses his legs or sits down."

With that, Jack turned to Jim and looked at him in disbelief. The thing is, Jim had only caught me looking. What he had not realized was that Jack and I, on more than one occasion, had indulged in a little mattress merriment together while Jim was at work.

"Fine. What do you want? I am sure that you realize that we don't always have a lot of choices," I conceded.

Jim studied me, probably wondering why I agreed so easily, and changed the subject so quickly. But bottom line, he wanted furniture and I had just told him that I could and would make it happen.

"I know that you will find just the perfect thing. How soon do you think we can have it?" Jim asked eagerly.

"These things don't magically appear," I answered with a cold stare. "I will need to do some scouting. Are you wanting to help or just let us do the work?"

"No, no, no, I don't steal," Jim said. "I will leave that up to you."

He might not steal but he had no problem with blackmail or taking in stolen goods.

"I will get on it right away and see what I can find," I said with resolve.

—•—

Bill and I were still trying to keep our relationship going but it was not easy. With our conflicting work schedules and no longer sharing a house, it seemed harder and harder to find opportunities to get together. And at times, it felt like he was making up excuses to avoid me.

However, during one of our times together Bill mentioned that he wished we had found a sofa for his living room. He was not happy with the hand-me-down left over from his college days, saying it was not his taste or even comfortable. I knew exactly what he would like and I knew where to find it — the condominium clubhouse by the pool at the development where Greg and I had hit two of the five models. But man, that would be crazy to even go back there. I felt that, most likely, they would have come up with some kind of security after our hit. Plus, I was sure by now that they had sold some of the units and people had moved in. But then I thought, *what could it hurt to just look?*

I mentioned this to Greg, who asked if I was nuts before saying, "Let's do it." Not knowing the situation or how things might have been altered since our last visit, we decided to go by in the daytime while there would be activity with the construction crews and such. We needed to get a feel for any changes that might have occurred. Then we could make a decision if the job would even be feasible. We drove through the complex first and did not spot anything out of the ordinary. The partially finished building from before looked completed and there were several cars in the parking spots by the clubhouse. In fact, we could see that there were even a couple of people by the pool so I parked and hoped that the clubhouse would be open. We found it unlocked with not a soul inside.

A Chippendale-style sofa, upholstered in navy faux-suede, sat in front of the fireplace along with a couple of end tables, lamps and two wingback chairs covered in a navy and burgundy floral linen. There were also two game tables, but not what we needed for Jim and Jack. I did not see any type of alarm system and figured that they would not have one. Most likely, the condo owners each had a key to the clubhouse. There were several ways to enter the main room besides the front entrance. Doors from the pool led directly into the clubhouse.

There were also doors to the restroom/changing rooms, which opened from the pool side and connected to the inside of the building. I made sure to unlock all of the doors and prayed that when we returned that at least one of them might not have been relocked.

When we got home, I called Bill and told him that I had found a sofa. A part of me wondered why I should even bother. However, another part of me rationalized that maybe we were just like those couples that tried to save their relationship by having a baby. I was trying to patch up what had now begun to feel like a "faux relationship" with a navy faux-suede sofa. How appropriate.

Bill had to work the late shift and could not help but offered us his car. I agreed that it would be easier to load than my sedan so I went by the restaurant and swapped cars with him.

Greg and I did not want to be too late since there were people living there now. We thought that maybe 8:30 might be a good time and headed back over, grateful to be in a different car. Sure enough, one of the doors to a changing room had been left unlocked. I was able to let myself in and then open the front doors for Greg. I had asked him earlier if there was anything that he wanted since he was helping me pick up something for Bill. I will always appreciate the fact that he said, "No, let's just get the sofa and get out of there."

I could not see anyone out and about and was thankful that the condo units did not directly face the clubhouse. We each picked up one end of the sofa and moved quickly through the double front doors to Bill's car. With a quick flip on its side, the sofa slid easily into the car and the tailgate closed. We got in and I started the car and pulled away.

As I drove down the hillside street, the engine sputtered and died. I tried to start the car again but no, it was dead. There we were, with the condominiums still in our rear view, in a car that would not start and a "hot" sofa in the back. We were both speechless.

"We need to get away from here," I said while trying not to panic. "I am going to put the car in neutral and coast to the bottom of the hill and then we will figure something out."

It was now a little after nine and we needed to call Bill. The station wagon had come to a stop at the bottom of the hill in front of a small house. There was a car in the drive and lights on inside and out.

"Stay here and I will go see if they will let me use their phone," I said to Greg.

The woman who answered the door could not have been nicer. She led me inside and pointed me to a pink Princess phone where I could make a call. I dialed the restaurant and asked for Bill and was told that he was busy.

"It is an emergency," I replied. A few moments later he got on the line.

"Hey, we have had car trouble. Can you come get us?" I was trying to not sound as scared as I was feeling.

"Is this before or after?" Bill asked in code.

"After," I replied. "You know, right down the hill from those condos that we talked about."

"Greg with you?" Bill asked.

"Yes."

"Is the car full?"

"Yes."

"I am on my way," he said.

I thanked my gracious hostess for the use of her phone and told her that my friend would arrive shortly. She offered to let me to wait inside but I assured her that I was fine waiting in my car and that I had a friend with me. She then said that if I needed anything else to just knock.

Bill arrived about 20 minutes later and immediately apologized for his car. I told him that it was not his fault.

"I have been having problems with the starter and should have told you. Sometimes if you jiggle it just right, it will work," Bill said.

"You have got to be kidding me. What if this had happened after we loaded the sofa and we were still in the complex parking lot?" I blurted out and felt a chill up my spine.

"I know, I know. I am so sorry. Let me see if I can get the car started so we can get out of here," he said, trying to appease me.

Surprisingly, he was able to cross his eyes and hold his tongue just right and start the car. I told him to drive it home and that I would drop off Greg and then come by and help him unload. Greg said that he would rather go with me to make sure Bill did not find himself stranded on the side of the road like we had – so we followed Bill home and unloaded the sofa.

"Can I get you something to drink?" Bill offered. "I really can't thank you both enough for doing this. Did you not get anything for yourselves?"

"No," said Greg abruptly. "Tonight was all about you and there wasn't any room in the car anyway."

"It's late, we need to be going," I sensed that this conversation would not get any better.

Once we got into my car, I braced myself for what was about to happen.

"You know that he is just using you. And don't think that I didn't notice all of the new things since the last time I was over there. You have been helping him steal, haven't you?" Greg asked.

What could I say? It was true, even the part about him using me. I had felt it too. I knew that I had to end whatever this was with Bill, and as calmly as possible, so that it did not come back to bite me in the ass.

"What are we going to do about Jim and Jack?" I asked deliberately changing the subject.

"What choice do we have? We need to find them a table and chairs and hey, I wouldn't mind a headboard for my guest room. My mom is coming in town for a few days next month," Greg said in a better mood.

I had always liked Greg's mom and looked forward to seeing her, as well as tasting her signature Chicken Cacciatore. She was not anything like Bill's hateful family.

A few days passed, and then a week, and then two. I kind of stopped calling Bill and he kind of stopped calling me. I decided that I needed some sort of closure so I broke down and called him at work just to say hello and make sure that he was doing okay. I figured that his dad was probably back in town and that he did not want me around any more than I wanted to be around him. Bill confirmed that his dad was there and apologized for losing touch. He sounded genuine when he asked if I was doing okay. That meant a lot to me. I still cared for him but now knew that the two of us together just would not work.

We ended the call by saying that we needed to get together sometime, knowing that we probably never would. However, it ended cordially and I did not fear any retribution from him and hoped that he felt the same.

—•—

My father decided to buy a new car for my mom and he gave me her 1968 Chevrolet Impala coupe. The car was already eight years old by then but had less mileage and it was in better condition than my Buick sedan. And while I was pleased to change cars, the thought did cross my mind that a two-door coupe would be harder to load and probably not hold as much as my previous car. Of course, I could not share that thought with my generous dad.

In the adjoining county, a new condo development was under construction. I saw an ad in the newspaper that stated their models were open "7 days a week" and were "Beautifully furnished by Palmer's Fine Furniture." Well, that certainly grabbed my attention. I decided that it was time to take a quick road trip.

I was blown away by the sheer size of the proposed development. There were a dozen buildings going up and acres of land cleared for more. Construction crews were everywhere but I did not see any cars in the parking area by either of the two model units. I was still leery that a salesman might be lurking inside. However, there was no one in the first unit as I made a quick pass. Bracing myself for someone in the second model, I approached the door and saw a sign that read "Back in a minute." The door was unlocked and I made another hasty run-through, checked everything out, unlocked a window and quickly left. I was going to slip back into the first model to also unlock a window, but now I saw movement where the drapes were parted and decided to go on before anyone took notice of me. If we were going to hit these units, it would be best if neither my car nor I had been spotted.

I called Greg as soon as I got home and said that I had found our next job and yes, there was something for Jim and Jack.

"Tonight?" Greg asked with a tinge of excitement.

"Yes, tonight." I answered. "I unlocked a window and I think we need to move fast."

It was nearly eleven when Greg rushed through the door where I was waiting for him. He'd had a situation at work that needed to be handled before he could leave. I explained my plan and asked if he was ready.

"Was there a headboard?" Greg asked hopefully.

"A wood one and a brass one in queen-size. And then a twin in the kid's bedroom," I explained.

"What else?" he asked eagerly.

I told him that I did not have time to stop and study everything, being fearful that a salesman might come in. But there was a velvet sofa that I would love and some really nice drapes and the usual chairs, tables and lamps.

"Oh, and there was a grandfather clock," I added.

I thought Greg was going to have an orgasm right then and there.

"I have always wanted a grandfather clock. Could I, I mean, could we get it and could I have it?" Greg asked hopefully.

I thought if I was going to ask for a sofa, the least that I could do would be to let Greg have the clock.

"Of course, but the main thing is the table and chairs to get Jim and Jack off our backs," I answered.

Greg had foolishly traded his Maverick in for a cute little VW Bug, which was totally worthless for moving furniture. And I was now driving the Chevy coupe, but at least it had a decent trunk. Needless to say, we took my car.

I was surprised at how something that had been such a flurry of activity earlier in the day was deader than dead as the clock approached midnight. The condos had garages, which made it difficult to see if anyone was at home. There were, however, a few houses with lights on. That made the hairs on the back of my neck stand at attention. Plus, my stomach began to do flips and I was grateful that I had started carrying plenty of Kleenex in my glove box.

The garage door was already up on the model unit. This caused me to have a moment of concern thinking "Why?" It made me question if we should pull into the garage and close the door as we had done in the past. I decided it might be better to park in an area away from the furnished models until we had everything ready to go.

The window was still unlocked, and I raised it, let myself in, and opened the back door for Greg. A lamp had been left on in two of the rooms. With draperies pulled back, it would be easy to spot us inside. I said that we needed to turn the lamps off and asked Greg if he already had an idea of what was in there and what he wanted before doing so. He said, "Yes" as we each turned off a lamp. It took a few minutes for our eyes to adjust but fortunately there were a couple of nearby streetlights that offered a glow so we were not in total darkness.

"I think the first thing to load would be the table and chairs. We can pack smaller things around them, but that is probably it for the first run," I explained.

I knew that Greg was anxious to load the grandfather clock in first. But we had no choice but to go for Jim and Jack's bribe. As usual, we gathered small items and placed them on the beds and then pulled the bedspreads around them. Once we were ready, I backed my car partially into the garage and opened the trunk for the dining table. I totally forgot that I had a concrete fruit stack in there, which I had picked up from a garden at a house earlier in the day. I hefted it out of the trunk and placed it in the garage and meant to pick it up later but never had the chance. Maybe the realtor thought of it as a lovely consolation prize!

With the table now in the trunk, the four chairs managed to fit in the backseat. Our bed linen-wrapped breakables were tucked in around them to keep everything from shifting. We were also able to load three lamps and a basket of accessories. I stacked the lampshades, hoping they would not get damaged, and placed them in Greg's lap for the ride home.

I wanted to bang on Jim and Jack's door and say, "Here's your friggin' table and chairs, assholes!" but decided to wait. I did not want to alert them to what was going on and I prayed that they were sound asleep. Now that we were aware that we had been loud when we had unloaded in the past, Greg and I moved in almost total silence as we gathered everything from my car.

On the way back out for the second load, I told Greg that I felt that we could get the clock and a headboard in the trunk together.

"What about your sofa?" Greg asked.

"It will have to be on another trip," I replied.

"Are you sure?" Greg asked in all seriousness.

It was ridiculous how much furniture we had already obtained in such a short period of time. So much so that our homes were overflowing. I wanted that sofa but certainly did not need it. I was fine with making sure that Greg got his clock and headboard first. All of a sudden I thought to myself, *when did I become so magnanimous?*

"What are you smiling at?" he asked.

"Nothing, just tired and being silly."

Everything looked just as we had left it – although I did notice that most of the neighbor's interior lights were now off. After all, it was after two AM – past everyone's bedtime.

I chose to park away from the model again until we had gathered more and were ready to load. Once that was done, I moved my car partially into the garage and we placed the grandfather clock into the trunk. We needed something to protect it so I took down a pair of draperies and covered it before placing the brass headboard on top. There was still a bit of room left and to keep everything from shifting, we gathered pillows, towels and even a shower curtain to stuff around it. Then we started to fill the back seat and found that we were able to place a pair of nightstands on the seat and the last of the lamps on the floorboard. A few pictures went in as well and then, once again, Greg sat in the front passenger seat holding lampshades.

I was so tired by the time we got back to our apartments and yet somehow we found the strength to silently unload everything and then carry Greg's new headboard upstairs. One thing we realized in loading the grandfather clock was that it did not have the heavy brass weights to make it work. It was still a handsome piece and I thought that we might be able to buy weights later on.

"Let's go," said Greg once the car was empty.

"Are you sure?" I asked. "It is after three now and I do not need to have the sofa. I know that you are every bit as exhausted as me."

"We're going. Don't argue," Greg stated.

"Okay. We'll put the sofa in the trunk and go. Neither one

of us needs anything else and I am not really sure that there is anything left to get," I told Greg.

This time around I pulled directly up to the unit. We carried the sofa to the car and almost dropped it twice. Once it was in the trunk, Greg started walking next door to the other model.

"Where are you going?" I said as quietly as possible. "Get back here." But he was determined and then started kicking down the back door off the enclosed patio of the second model. I got there just as he walked inside.

"Are you crazy? You are going to get us arrested," I yelled as loud as I could in a whisper.

"Hurry. Start grabbing things. We don't have much time," Greg demanded.

For once, I did as he told me and started carrying things to the car. Cram, stuff, squeeze another thing or two inside. We were busting at the seams and still, he was carrying out a small chair.

"There is no way in hell that is going to fit," I said.

"Yes, it will. In the front seat," Greg replied.

"And where are you planning on riding?" I asked, as he got in the car and scrunched down on the floorboard.

"Put the chair in the seat and let's go," he instructed.

I did as he requested and then jumped in the car and drove away. We both started laughing from the sheer exhaustion as well as the craziness of everything. Greg was crammed on the floor between the dash and the seat.

"Hurry. Get me home," he pleaded.

The clock on the dashboard of my coupe was inching its way towards four AM as we drove toward the city. Ahead I could see the faint glow in the sky of city lights as we crossed back over the county line. The darkness and stillness seemed to engulf us. Although we were driving on a main artery into town, at this time of the morning rush hour had not begun. Homes sat far back from the road and their exterior floodlights, like the stars in the clear night sky, sparkled in the deep murkiness of the morning.

Greg and I had now been on several late night adventures. The outcome had left us with beautifully furnished homes. We were often asked how we could afford these luxuries and with some very creative storytelling (I always thought I was the most convincing) we would each spin our tales.

Now, here we were in the early hours of the morning headed home from our third and final trip from Creekview. My trunk was flung open wide with half of a velvet sofa hanging out – complete with tags still attached.

Way off in the distance, a pair of headlights was coming toward us. There was no need to be alarmed. But as we continued to move closer and closer, I felt an explosion in my stomach. I realized that it was not just any other car. It was, in fact, a police car.

I yelled to Greg but from down on the floorboard he was unable to move, much less see what I saw. The police car slowed down a bit as it passed – but at least it passed us and kept going. However, before I could catch my breath, I saw the car make a U-turn. Then shattering the darkness, the lights on its roof began flashing.

I will always credit Greg for what happened next. In the past, I had been the voice of reason. However, I panicked and said that I needed to outrun them. I knew the neighborhoods and for a split second I thought, like most stupid criminals, that I could lose them.

"No," yelled Greg. That one word snapped me out of my hysteria.

I pulled my car over and took a deep breath. One of the officers, the driver, got out of the car and approached my window, which I had already rolled down in anticipation. He asked for my license and registration and where we were headed.

"Home," I replied. He then walked around the car and using his flashlight, peered through the windows, and studied the tags hanging off the rust-velvet, tufted-back sofa, which appeared to be trying to escape from my trunk.

He asked about the furnishings and that is when I turned in an Academy-Award-worthy performance. I explained that I had just rented my first apartment and then shared how my parents had purchased furniture for me and given me pieces from our family home. I explained that this was my last load. I said that I had hoped to start moving earlier in the evening but that I had gotten off work late. I finished with how excited I was to finally move out of my parents' home.

I was not sure if he was buying my explanation but he did listen before taking my driver's license back to his vehicle. Greg was impressed by my performance and said he knew all along that I would probably be able to lie my way out of whatever trouble might find us. I quickly shushed him as I saw both police officers exit the car and head our way. I was fearful that someone had already called in the robbery.

The second officer approached the window and asked if I attended the local college. I said that I had, but graduated a couple of years back. He said that he thought that my name had sounded familiar and that he had graduated from the same college three years earlier. It dawned on him that, yes, I had been the school's beaver mascot. He told his partner that he knew me and was sure that all was fine.

With that, the first officer gave me back my license and said that we could go.

"Be careful and, hey, congratulations on your new home," added the other officer.

Greg was relieved, thinking that we had avoided an arrest, but in my mind I quickly raced through the various scenarios, all of which led back to us getting caught. The robbery would be discovered as soon as the day began. The county police would be called to investigate and most likely begin canvassing the area. Did someone see my car coming and going in the early morning hours? And more importantly, did someone at the complex catch my license tag number?

I was not sure how the County Police system worked but I assumed that they would notify the City Police Department. That could mean that the officers who stopped us would become suspicious. My imagination ran wild and by the time we had arrived back at our apartment complex, I had worked out a plan. Since the police never asked for Greg's name, we quickly unloaded our final haul into his apartment and then rushed to move the other recently stolen items out of my apartment. We did not take the time to load them back into my car but simply carried everything across the parking lot and stacked them wherever we could find room in Greg's home. The sun was beginning to peek across the horizon as we finished and I needed to shower and get ready for work.

I don't think that I had ever been as scared as I was then. My life was about to end. The embarrassment that it would cause my family would be something that we would never come back from. And yet, I had told a convincing lie to a policeman who thought that he knew me and all of a sudden everything was okay. Two and two somehow did not add up to an arrest.

With absolutely no sleep, paranoia had set in. I could barely function all day at work. But the police did not come that day or the next. The days turned into weeks and those weeks turned into a month. Finally, I allowed myself to breathe and accept that we might have gotten away with it. We were free. We had been rewarded with three packed carloads of stolen expensive furniture and accessories. We were invincible!

If that were true, then I was ready to divide our treasures and enjoy the fruits of our labor.

—●—

For the few weeks after that earth-shattering night, Greg and I avoided Jim and Jack. We had their table and chairs, but we were hesitant to give anything to them until we were sure that the police would not be coming for us. Finally, a month later, when it appeared that the Creekview fiasco was behind us, we moved the table and chairs out of Greg's back door and carried it just a few feet to place them on Jim and Jack's patio. We then knocked on their sliding glass door and took a seat.

They were stunned, surprised and excited by the rattan dining set with the butterfly laminate top and quickly moved it inside. The four of us fixed drinks and sat down to admire. Somehow we had managed not to wake them the night of the close call. It was a miracle that we did we not attract attention unloading three carloads, as well as moving pieces from my apartment across the parking lot to Greg's apartment in the early morning hours – all the while, fearful that the police were on their way to arrest us. It was funny how that event, which caused several sleepless nights, was now just a distant memory. Everything seemed right with the world again.

"So where are you going to say that you found your new dinette set?" I asked.

"Friend of a friend," said Jim with a devilish grin.

"It damn well better not be these friends. Because these friends are not risking everything again," I said with a bit of attitude.

"I have always liked the name Nathaniel," said Jack, realizing that he needed to step in. "I will just say that my friend Nathaniel was moving and made me a deal that was too good to pass up."

"Nathaniel? Hmm... Nathaniel and the Midnight Movers. I like it," added Greg.

"Me too," I agreed.

You are probably thinking that we had learned our lesson after that ordeal and close call.

Sorry, but you would be mistaken.

—•—

Greg's new brass headboard was in place in his spare bedroom. One of the bedspreads that had been used to protect the breakables now covered the bed. I had helped to arrange accessories and hang the artwork. Fresh flowers were sitting on the dresser and Greg was off to pick up his mom at the airport.

He had asked if I could hang out since I think he was a little nervous at her seeing everything. There had been such a drastic change in his apartment since her last visit with the influx of expensive furnishings filling every room. I was happy to be there waiting for them to arrive. We had planned later to take her out to dinner.

Her reaction was strained when she saw everything. I thought that she might just be tired. However, Greg's apartment was clearly bathed in extravagance – things that a 26-year-old most likely would not be able to afford.

"Where did all of this come from?" she asked her son.

"Don't you like it, mom? I tried to fix everything up nice for your visit," Greg was trying to mask his disappointment at her bewilderment.

"You can't afford this. I can only imagine the debt that you are in right now," she said before turning to me and adding, "I am sure it was you who talked him into spending all of this money."

"Sure, I helped him pick out some things. But he is doing so well at his job that he wanted to dress his place up a bit," I said coming to Greg's defense.

Quickly I saw that I was not being helpful.

"We did not raise him to be like this. So pretentious. It is all your doing," Greg's mom said staring at me.

Oh my God, another parent thinking that I had ruined their child.

"I am so sorry. Maybe I should go," I said apologetically, before adding, "I hope that you have a nice visit."

Greg looked stunned. I knew that he wanted to apologize to me but I shook my head. He needed to make things right with his mom. Neither of us could have predicted her reaction.

I had been to his parent's home during a spring break once and remembered that it was humble, comfortable and nothing fancy. Greg's place was far nicer than his mom's home. Maybe it was jealousy or maybe, if she thought that he had bought everything, then there was no way to think that her son was not in serious debt. And neither one of us could tell her the truth. So Greg let her believe that he had gone in debt to acquire everything.

"Let me show you to your room. It has new sheets and everything," said Greg to his mom as I opened the door to leave.

"I am not an idiot. I know what new sheets feel like," Greg's mom said in a huff.

Yikes.

Chapter Eight

"Dean broke up with Karen," Greg said when I picked up the phone.

"Well, that lasted longer than any of us thought possible. Did she discover those Polaroids of him in drag?" I replied with my best snark.

"You are such a bitch," he said, giggling.

"Part of my charm," I replied.

"God, he did make an ugly woman, didn't he?" Greg said reflectively.

"Now who is the bitch?" I asked while trying to keep a straight face.

We both started laughing, not so much at our former roommate's romantic plight but at the reminder of that night – the night Dean had decided to perform in drag. It was not a pretty sight. Dean was comical and yet that was not his intention.

Plus it did not help that I had a short-lived successful run as a drag performer at a local gay bar. Now, as for Greg, he never tried performing in drag in public but he had no problem wrapping himself up in a shower curtain and lip-synching the 1969 hit *Spirit in the Sky* as he danced in circles around our living room.

Finally Greg got to the point of his call and told me that Dean needed a place to live.

"Are you letting him move in?" I inquired.

"Yes, and no. I have an idea," Greg said excitedly.

It turned out that Greg worked with someone who had just moved into a new apartment complex nearby and he thought that the three of us might want to check it out and possibly move back in together. I was not sure that I wanted two roommates again but I did remember all of the fun that we had in the past.

"What about our furnishings? Won't he suspect something? Or does he already know?" I asked hoping that Greg had kept his mouth shut.

Dean had been out of our lives for a while. He had moved in with a girlfriend and pretty much distanced himself from us. Other than the occasional lunch or dinner, neither one of us had spent much time with him. Plus, as it turned out, he had not been to our homes since we had redecorated from the *Midnight Run Bargain Boutique*. There is no way he would believe that either of us had made enough money to buy everything in that short period of a time. I did not think that the "friend of a friend" explanation would fly with Dean.

"I am curious but not saying 'yes.' Still, I would be willing to take a look," I informed Greg. "I am not making any commitments until we have a chance to sit down with Dean and make sure that we have some ground rules."

That was all Greg needed to hear. He asked if I could go after work that day and check it out. Our work schedules had changed. Greg had a new job at a bank with regular banking hours. I was doing freelance interior design work from another designer's workroom. My hours were somewhat flexible. I realized that I did not even know what Dean was doing these days. The last I heard was that he worked for an optical company. It is strange how you can be so close to someone and then lose touch like that.

The three of us met at the apartment complex's office where we were then directed to take a look at a three-bedroom, two-bath, second-floor unit. I have to say, brand new is really nice and I found the spacious layout desirable. I had already made up my mind that I would be willing to pay, once again, a little extra just to have the master bedroom with the private bath. Greg and Dean would each have separate bedrooms but they would have to share the hall bath.

The decor was Harvest Gold carpet, wallpaper and appliances. No chocolate-brown lusciousness, but at least the apartment was new and we would be the first to occupy that unit. Dean and I fell back into a groove as old friends do and I thought that we could make this work. I said yes and we all signed on the dotted line. Two weeks later we moved into our new place.

Greg had let go of his plastic Mediterranean bedroom furniture. Since my bedroom furniture matched my parents, I gave them my triple dresser to go with their suite, as they had only purchased the tall chest on chest. I kept the extra nightstand to use as an end table.

I had also changed my color palette to the more trendy peach and blue colors, after having found a beautiful, quilted-chintz comforter in ivory with peach and blue flowers along with a peach dust ruffle. I had taken it from the same unit where my rust velvet sofa had once lived, along with a cane back armchair that had a rust and peach flame stitch cushion. Greg still loved his jungle green color scheme from the previous apartment with the brass headboard he had obtained just in time for his mom's disastrous visit. He added his painted credenza and a black lacquered chinoiserie coffee table to the overall design theme for our living room. His large yellow floral oil painting now hung over my sofa.

Dean did not have much in the way of furniture since he had moved in with the last girlfriend and shared her fully-furnished home. But fortunately, the god-awful plaid sofa bed had finally bitten the dust somewhere along the way. He was more than happy that Greg and I had a few extra pieces, including my leftover headboard. And as it turned out, Dean had no problem letting us decorate his bedroom.

Greg and I did not come fully clean about our furniture. Greg had a decent job and salary. It could almost be believed that he could at least afford a down payment on everything. And I worked as an interior designer, with an interior design shop. So naturally, I could buy things wholesale, making it all somewhat plausible. I think that Dean was happy to have an attractive home and did not pursue the conversation much beyond what he was told. Our arrangement lasted for about seven months and then Dean met someone and gave us notice.

"That S.O.B. We should have known he would do this to us. Again," I told Greg in a royally pissed-off tone.

"So, what do you want to do?" Greg asked much more calmly.

"I think that I can swing the rent difference if you can. I would rather not move, plus we are stuck with a year's lease," I replied dialing back my tirade because Greg was not to blame.

"Well, at least we don't need to buy any furniture!" he said with a chuckle.

The two of us stayed on in that apartment for the remainder of the year and the year after that. We had it beautifully furnished but when we would find something new, we would sell off older pieces to make room – some of those extras even found their way to my parents' home.

Eventually my mom and dad began to question how I could afford everything.

My parents asked me to come over for dinner one night. That was not an unusual request but once I got there, I realized that they had something on their minds. It had been ten years since I had given them that Hepplewhite console and octagon commode table while I was in high school. However, in the last couple of years, I had also given them two chairs, two tables, three lamps and some artwork. I don't think their first thought was that they had raised a thief, but having visited our overly furnished apartment had raised questions regarding my finances. They, like Bill and Greg's parents, had concluded that I was going deep into debt buying these things. And while they appreciated their gifts, they thought that it was too much.

It was time to take the *Nathaniel and the Midnight Movers* story out for a spin.

"Son, we're worried about you," my dad began.

"And don't think that we don't appreciate your generosity," tag-teamed my mother.

"But how can you afford all of these beautiful things?" added my dad.

"We're afraid that you're digging yourself in a hole and that you'll never get out of debt," said my mom, adding, "I mean, we had to save for several years just to buy our dining room suite."

I told my parents that Nathaniel, someone Greg knew from back when he worked at the motel, would often have furniture and stuff for sale at really low prices. I went on to say that even though we all suspected, no one really wanted to know the truth.

"We just assumed that it might have 'fallen off of a truck' somewhere. And several of Greg's fellow employees were buying things, too," I replied. "So we did not feel as if it was that big of a risk to us. I'll stop if you think that I should."

"Well, you don't know for sure that it is stolen," said my dad after a long pause.

Was that a question or was he stating a fact? Anyway, that was all I needed to continue. Plus there were "Nathaniel" pieces of furniture, lamps and artwork scattered throughout their home as well as my dad's office. If they acknowledged everything was stolen and asked me to stop, then they would probably feel like they needed to get rid of all of the things that they already had. Wouldn't that be illegal? Selling stolen goods? It was the basic Catch-22.

No one would have ever believed the sheer volume of inventory we all had accumulated since my first run a decade ago. The apartment that Greg and I shared was overflowing. Bill had a bunch of things as well as my parents. I assumed that Jim and Jack still had their rattan dinette set with the butterfly laminate top although Greg and I had lost touch with them after our move. Things had never felt right once they had blackmailed us. Oh, and we can't forget the items which we had for a brief while and then sold or gave away. Absolutely incredible! We never stopped our midnight moving excursions, although we would take breaks now and then.

—•—

The second time our apartment lease came up, Greg and I both knew that we did not want to renew. It had been a fun place over the past two years but it was now time to move on. My business was growing but Greg had reached burnout with his bank job. He was talking about moving back to his hometown to be near family.

No more apartments for me. I ended up buying a condo! It was in a new complex though not the quality of the developments where we had *shopped* late at night. Still, it was what I could afford and on the good side of town. They only had one furnished model. I felt like such a snob, but there really wasn't anything in it that I thought worth stealing. Of course, even I would not dare to steal where I lived.

Greg did move out of state and it took a while to get used to the idea of him not being around. He moved all of his furnishings, including the grandfather clock. It was now working since we had obtained the missing brass weights. Greg and I found the balls to go into Palmer's Fine Furniture where the clock had come from just a few weeks after cleaning out their furnished model at Creekview. I thought that if they had another clock on the floor with the weights, then we might be able to steal them. And when I say, weights, I mean heavy-ass brass cylinders. We needed three but there was no way to get all of them out of the store in just one trip. However, I realized that it would too be risky to make multiple trips.

There was indeed a similar clock on the second floor with all three weights hanging from brass chains behind a glass and wood door. The key was in the lock allowing me to open the case. I took one weight off the chain and set it on the cushion of a nearby sofa.

"We need to get one of these weights downstairs and near the door," I explained. "Then we can each put a weight in our pants and walk out with it. I will run back in and grab the third weight, and then we will get away from the store as fast as possible."

I put one weight in my pants and awkwardly walked around pretending to be shopping as I descended the back stairs and made my way toward a room setting near the front of the store. I needed to be careful. There were times that I brought clients there to shop and did not want anyone there to suspect me of theft.

I slipped the weight out of my pants, tucked it behind a chair cushion, and went back upstairs. Greg had removed the other two weights and had them ready.

"It's not easy walking with that much in your pants," I said with a smile.

"You talking from experience?" Greg asked while trying his best not to crack up.

"I have never had any complaints," I said confidently.

"Okay, now you're just bragging," Greg said. "Although I am not a size queen, I can be impressed!"

Before I could laugh I saw a salesman out of the corner of my eye walking our way. The brass weights were still in plain view on the sofa so I quickly walked toward the salesman. I directed him away by expressing interest in a chair in a distant room display. By the time I had returned, Greg had hidden one weight in the pillows and had the other already in his pants.

"You are right. I am afraid to even move. It feels like it is going to drop down my pants' leg," said Greg.

"Did you put it in your underwear?" I asked. "That's what I had to do."

Greg looked at me like I was an idiot.

Once we both had our pants packed we walked downstairs very gingerly and out the front door. Anyone watching us would think that we were destined for a career in porn with the bulges that we were displaying.

After we had unloaded the two weights into my car, I ran back inside, almost colliding with the salesman from my earlier encounter.

"I am so sorry, but do you have a restroom?" I asked.

He smiled and pointed off to the side and I excused myself. It was now or never. I waited for a few moments, flushed and prayed that no one would be near the front of the store when I came out.

I exited the restroom and headed back toward the front entrance where a couple had just come through the door. I saw that the salesman was walking toward them. They must have asked for something specific because he stretched out his arm and motioned for them to follow. I smiled as they passed and then quickly snatched up the weight, slid it down my pants and adjusted the pillow that had obscured it earlier. I thought that was the most action that my pants and I have had in a while.

Greg was watching my every move from the front seat of the car as I exited the store. He saw the look of panic on my face as I realized the weight was headed south. There was nothing to do but grab my crotch, hold it and keep walking. I was relieved to remove the weight from my pants once I sat down in the car. We had successfully taken three heavy brass cylinder weights from a grandfather clock located upstairs in a fine furniture store in the middle of the day – now it was time to head home.

With the weights installed and the clock freshly wound, the pendulum began to swing back and forth. But the loud ticking sound echoing through his apartment caused Greg to make a face.

"Don't even," I said before he could complain. "You wanted it, now you are going to have to live with it!"

Chapter Nine
present day

"Are you pleased with how everything is going?" asked Roberta Ann.

My moving sale had been a flurry of activity so far and she wanted to make sure that I was not upset as I watched people haul away the things that I had collected over the years. What she did not realize was that it never really was mine to begin with.

"Everyone is enjoying your stories. I think that they are buying some of the pieces simply because of the way you talk about them. Everyone loves knowing the history. I will admit that I was not on board at first with having you here during the sale but it has been a big plus. We are making a killing."

I watched as a young couple looked at, and then sat on, one of my sofas. It had been covered in velvet at one time, sticking out of the trunk of my Chevy coupe when the police pulled us over in the early morning hours. *Hmm, maybe that little morsel was something I needed to keep to myself.*

The sofa was top quality and the shape was classic. I had decided several years ago to invest in reupholstering it in a stunning coral Jacquard fabric. I had always loved that color and knew that it would be just the punch I needed for my living room with my signature cobalt blue lacquered walls. It was at one time a very dramatic room but has since been painted neutral at the request of my realtor.

"Drama doesn't sell. People need a clean, fresh slate," said my realtor.

He might just as well have said, "Make it bland. You can never go wrong with boring." *When did I become so out of vogue? I had always been known for my excellent taste.*

The couple started walking my way as I looked up from my chair.

"Do you have a question?" I asked.

"We love that sofa. It is so retro," the man replied.

Jeez. Retro? Clearly I have been around so long that I am coming back into style.

"It is a classic," I said. "And the fabric is in excellent condition. I have taken very good care of it over the years."

I managed to refrain from telling them the number of drinks that had been spilled on it, my old lover passed out drunk or the number of times that I have had sex on it. Yes, some things are best kept to myself. I mean, that is the real reason it had to be reupholstered. If only those cushions could talk... well, it would be X-rated. But still, there are some memories that will always be scorched into my brain.

"Are you okay? Are you too hot out here? Your face is so red," the customer asked with concern.

Blush, I never blush. I can't imagine what it would take to make me blush. Maybe it really is the heat.

I assured them that I was fine.

"Should I get someone to help you load it into your car?" I asked.

— ● —

"We have an offer for the dining table but they don't need the chairs," said Roberta Ann walking over to me. "Would it be okay to split them up?"

Funny, I had just been remembering that night and the where and how I had latched on to those pieces. I had considered getting a different table at one point simply to change it up and not be so obvious, but I never did because the set of chairs complimented the drop leaf table so well that I just could not bring myself to do it.

"I am fine with that. Surely someone will need and appreciate the chairs," I answered.

Of course, young people just don't do much in the way of formal entertaining anymore. My moving sale folks had already warned me that my collection of silver would most likely not be in demand. No one wants to polish silver. I couldn't argue with that but I do still remember how spectacular my parties would be with tray after silver tray of delicious mouth-watering hors d'oeuvres.

The dining table did sell and later that day someone bought the set of eight chairs at a much more discounted price that I had ever imagined. But then again, I had not paid anything for them so I guess I still came out ahead. Plus, I had many years of use. The antique lowboy also found a home as did the mirror that had hung over it for so long. Slowly but surely, everything was being carried away. Well, at least it was not happening in the middle of the night.

—●—

"Look honey, a conch shell. Oh, never mind, it's fake," said a woman perusing a table of my objet d'art. That was all it took to snap me out of my daydream.

"I am sorry, but that is not for sale," I quickly said.

"Fine. We didn't want it anyway," said the young woman who I found myself being mesmerized by her oversized pointy breasts. "It's not a real shell and I like things that are natural."

I thought to myself that she must be kidding. Seriously, natural? I was dying to say to her: *You mean like those flotation devices you are proudly displaying in that low cut t-shirt? You could put someone's eye out with them.* But once again, I showed restraint.

"Yes, I know it's not real but it has sentimental value to me. It was a gift and was not supposed to be in the sale," I explained.

"Someone gave you a fake shell? Why?" she foolishly continued.

"Because they could," I said sharply.

"But it's so tacky," she had the audacity to say. *Oh no, she did not just go there, did she?*

"Well, if anyone should know tacky..." *Yikes, did I just say that out loud? Now what?*

"What's that supposed to mean?" she said in a huff.

I was already in so deep, so why not continue?

"It means that you clearly do not have a mirror at home or you would not go out in public dressed like that. You talk about fake, well, there is nothing real about your boobies," I snapped and then decided to continue since I was on a roll. "And while I am talking about your appearance, how did you manage to style your hair like that? Did you stick your head in a blender and hit frappe?"

She had a stunned look on her face and was trying to find a clever comeback when Roberta Ann came over.

"Ricky, may I see you over here for just a minute," she calmly asked.

"I am so sorry, she just irritated me. I will apologize," I said once we had moved away from Debbie Double-D.

"Don't apologize on my account. I have had to deal with her at other sales. She is a pill. Always criticizing things then wanting a big discount," said Roberta Ann. "Personally, I was enjoying your little exchange but then I noticed that there were others listening in and I thought I better pull the plug before we lost customers."

"I will try to behave. Thank you," I said apologetically.

"Oh no, thank you for the entertainment!" Roberta Ann said with a wicked smile.

Chapter Ten

Bill was now back in my life. Well, not as a lover but as a friend. He knew someone in need of an interior designer and thought of me. That someone, as it turned out, was his latest love. And I mean L-O-V-E. I had never seen Bill so head over heals, batshit crazy in love. I certainly never saw him that way when we were together. At first it was a bit hurtful, but honestly, I did not want him back and was sincerely grateful just to reconnect as friends.

His new love had recently separated from his boyfriend and was left with the home that the two of them had shared. The apartment was in serious need of a facelift and Bill thought that I could help. The new beau, Dan, was a cutie and very flirtatious. I was not sure that Bill was seeing everything clearly but I picked up on it immediately. Dan was now free and not quite ready to settle down. Bill, on the other hand, was already picking out china patterns.

The apartment was the second floor of an old historic home on a prime street. I agreed that it was worth a makeover.

Bill definitely had his own ideas but he thought by having me assist that I could act as a buffer. This would allow them to keep their relationship on track and not get bogged down in the disagreements that can often happen during renovations.

"Well, it is what I do," I said.

The other interesting part of the equation was that Bill's father had decided to retire and move to town permanently. And since he owned the house where Bill lived, then why not share it with his son? That was too much for Bill. I knew that he felt that his only way out of that situation would be to move in with Dan. Yeah, karma's a bitch.

So we had a plan – redecorate Dan's apartment and make it suitable for the new couple. I was not sure Dan was 100% on board with that plan. But financially, Dan was going to need a roommate. As it turned out, Dan really did not have a steady job and Bill was more or less financing him. I will admit that Dan and the apartment were probably worth the investment.

Did I mention that Dan was flirtatious?

I had to be careful because Bill picked up on Dan's flirting with me and I wanted to be professional. *Oh, who am I kidding?* I knew something was going to happen. It was just a matter of time.

New paint and wallpaper made a huge difference in their apartment. Actually, just cleaning it made a huge difference. Once that was done, we began moving some of Bill's things over and a few of Dan's things out the door. Dan did not have any attachment to the dorm-quality items that he owned. Plus he was smart enough to know Bill's pieces were definitely a cut above.

Bill felt that he had to leave some of his furniture, along with the custom rug, with his father. It appeared that his father felt the same. When I thought about it, I got angry imagining that S.O.B. enjoying things that Bill would never have had without me. But, why go there?

Dan called me at the design studio one day and asked if I wanted to come over for dinner.

"Sure, would love to," I said accepting his offer. Bill had graduated from being a restaurant manager and had opened his own small catering business. He was a good cook so I expected a nice meal. However, when I got there, Bill was not at home. Dan said Bill was catering. So Dan had picked up Chinese takeout for us. *Interesting.* We had not been alone before, at least not for any period of time.

The two of us enjoyed our Moo Shu Pork with hot and sour soup and egg rolls. Conversation was easy and among other things, we talked about the next step in decorating his place.

Did I mention that Dan was flirtatious?

He smiled, laughed and stroked my leg all through dinner. Then his hand began to move its way up my thigh, headed towards my fortune cookie. *Uh oh. Bill who?*

Dan said that he had some ideas for the bedroom and thought that we needed to take a look. His ideas just happened to be clothing optional. *Oh, the sacrifices I have had to make just to keep my clients happy.*

"Dinner was nice but it could not compare to dessert," I said later as I rolled over to face Dan.

"I hoped that you would like that. I have been wanting to say thanks for everything that you have done in helping me with the apartment," he replied.

"I must admit that was an extremely nice thank you note," I continued.

"It won't be the last," Dan purred.

With that, he looked at the clock and said Bill would probably be home soon and that he needed to clean up. I offered to help but Dan thought it would be best if I did not stay. I understood, thanked him again and went on my way thinking, that was an interesting evening for sure.

"I hear you and Dan had dinner," Bill said when he called me the next day. I was not sure how much he knew about the menu from the previous night but if he did suspect something had happened, he did not let on.

"Dan thinks you are wonderful and loves what you have done with the place," he continued.

"He is a great guy. You are very lucky and I am so happy for the two of you," I said.

I thought to myself, *I am such a lousy friend but then, Bill was a lousy lover. So does that make us even?*

—●—

Once the renovations were done, Bill officially moved out of the house that he shared with his father and into Dan's apartment. Their home looked infinitely better than when I first saw it, but it was in need of a few more things.

"I would like to go on a midnight run with you," Bill blurted out one day shortly after he moved in.

"You are kidding, Bill? Tell me that you are kidding," I implored.

"No, I am dead serious. You know that we could use a couple of chairs and I would love something for that wall in the dining room," he continued.

"And what about Dan? No way in hell are we dragging him into this," I said firmly.

"I already have," Bill replied.

He told me that he and Dan had scouted out a couple of places. But the only thing that they had picked up was a pair of concrete obelisks from a patio somewhere. He went on to say that Dan was fine with everything and wanted to do more. Bill then told me that he had shared with Dan where most of his furniture came from.

"You told him about me?" I asked in disbelief.

"Not so much that you found and planned everything. But that together we ran across a few things," said Bill.

I was not sure what made me the most angry. The fact that he had told my secrets or that he actually was trying to take credit.

"No."

"What do you mean, no? Come on Ricky – or should I say, Nathaniel?" Bill pleaded.

"Don't even. I am pissed."

"Do I need to send Dan over to convince you?" he said in a sexy voice.

Does he know what he is saying? Does he know that Dan and I have, well, you know? Or does he just think Dan might be able talk me into it?

"Or would you prefer the two of us coming over to convince you?" he murmured.

"Did you just suggest a three-way?" I asked.

"Is that what it would take?" Bill cooed.

I wanted to say no and act insulted, but instead I felt a tingle in the jingle.

"Let me think about it," I replied.

A week later I had found something promising but was already having second thoughts about it. It was a condominium but not a furnished model or clubhouse. I joined Dan and Bill for dinner at their home – and yes, this time they were both there. I started to explain and Bill jumped in before I had finished.

"I'm in. Whatever it is," said Bill excitedly.

"Give me a minute. You need to know the details," I said.

Yes, it was another new condo development in a good area. They had not furnished their model except to set it up as an office. The clubhouse was small and, while I would not turn down some of the pieces, there was nothing to get worked up about. However, in looking through the windows of some of the empty units, I found one that was not empty.

Now, I am not one to break into someone's home while they are living there but this appeared to be storage. Most likely they had purchased the unit, stacked all of their furniture in it and planned on moving in later. What I could see through the windows was spectacular. Elegant antique chests and tables stacked everywhere. A pair of burgundy damask covered Louis IV armchairs were in plain view and I could only imagine what else that unit held.

"Sounds perfect," said Bill.

"No, it's not. These are clearly someone's personal furnishings. They could be family pieces. They do not look like the mass produced furniture store brands. These are fine antiques," I stated.

"You are getting me excited," Bill said flirtatiously.

"Bill, listen. This crosses the line. You have got to be sure that you want to cross it," I insisted.

"I hear you and I am telling you, I am okay with it," he replied.

I felt that I had to process what he had just said. He was fine with essentially breaking into someone's home and stealing their furniture. Granted, no one lived there. Still, it was not only risky but what if we actually knew the people? And then I thought, *if I had such a problem with it, why did I even bring it to their attention? What does that say about me?* Clearly I did not have any reservations either.

"Dan, what about you?" I asked.

"I trust you guys and it sounds amazing," he answered.

"Okay," I said with a nod of my head.

"Okay?" Bill repeated.

"Yes," I answered. And with that, Bill leaned over and kissed me hard on the mouth followed by Dan doing the same thing. *Was he really serious about a three-way? That would only complicate things.* I was disappointed and relieved when they both backed away.

"When?" asked Bill.

"Can we go tonight?" inquired Dan.

"Why not?" I replied.

—•—

The wonderful thing about Bill being in the catering business was that he now drove a panel van. Of course, it was ideal for loading furniture but I felt that it was also more conspicuous when circling a neighborhood or parked outside of someone's home. I suggested that we take my car along with the van, but that we park his vehicle in a nearby church's lot and retrieve it when we were sure everything was clear and ready to load.

There was one other possible kink in our plan. We did not know if the condo had an alarm system. It was the late 1970s and alarms were beginning to pop up here and there. Usually there would be a sticker in the window or a small sign in the yard, but this unit had neither. We were not sure what to do about a silent alarm, but we did know to run like hell if an alarm siren ever pierced the night.

I had encountered an alarm recently when I went into an empty house that was for sale. I did not notice any alarm company signage from outside and a window happened to be unlocked. I let myself in, walked around checking out the lighting and hardware but did not see anything worth taking. It is funny how opinionated and picky I had become. But instead of going back out through the window, I unlocked the exterior door closest to my car and walked out. By the time I was opening my car door, I heard the alarm, cursed like a sailor and raced out of there. Now I was wondering, what if this condo has an alarm like that?

The front door was locked, as were the ground floor windows. We walked around to the back and unlatched the tall gate that led into the patio area. I was grateful for the six-foot high fencing that gave us some cover. The back windows and pair of French doors were also locked. It was going to have to be a bump and grind or we'd break a window. For some reason, I have found that bumping a pair of doors is easier than a single door. Often they are not bolted at the top or bottom and simply give way to the pressure, which was the case that night.

We were now inside and waiting to see if an alarm went off. So far nothing. Still learning about this added inconvenience, I had found that the alarm keypads were usually by a garage or exterior door. I took a quick tour and held my breath when I spotted an alarm panel by the door leading out to the garage. Panic was about to set in until I realized that it had a green light on. No one had set the alarm. There was no flashing red light. I was thankful for their carelessness.

"We are okay," I said stepping back into the room.

Then all of a sudden I had a horrific thought. *What if someone had moved in and just had not arranged their furniture? They could be upstairs in one of the bedrooms right now.*

"I am going to check upstairs," I said, not wanting to worry them until I knew for sure. My legs were trembling as I ascended the staircase, stopped on the landing to listen, and then continued upward. There were only two bedrooms upstairs and the doors were open wide. I could see that the rooms were empty, thanks to the moonlight coming through the windows. But just to make sure, I also checked both baths. I needed to know that no one was hiding from me.

"Empty," I disclosed as I came back downstairs.

Bill nodded and started pointing at everything. He was practically giddy with excitement. He then sat in one of the French chairs.

"Mine," he said.

"Don't even start calling dibs. Let's just get as much as we can and then divide it up," I instructed.

There was a half flight of steps leading down to the garage level. I unhooked the 8' wide garage door so that it could be opened manually. We started carrying chairs, tables, chests, lamps and rugs, stacking them where we could. It was a one-car garage, so there was no way to fill it with everything and then park inside as well.

Behind a few tall clothing boxes, I found a drop-leaf dining room table laying on its side.

"Mine," I said.

"I thought that you said we couldn't call dibs," stated Bill.

"Changed my mind," I replied with a smile.

Dan helped me carry my new dining table to the garage. Then I focused on the eight Chippendale side chairs. It took two of us to move the antique chests, French chairs and rugs. The garage was filling up so fast that I could not imagine how many trips we might have to make just to get everything home. It was time to retrieve the van. I drove Bill back to the church where he jumped in his vehicle, followed me over and then parked in front of the garage. I parked my car a couple of doors down, ready to move it once we had Bill's van packed.

The French chairs and dining table went in first. There was still room for one of the chests and three rolled-up Oriental rugs went on top. A couple of small tables also fit and two of my dining room chairs turned upside down. That was it.

"I will take the van back to the church lot and wait. You and Dan load your car and then meet me," said Bill.

We had a plan. I moved my car and was determined that the remaining dining room chairs would make it into the trunk and back seat. With every job, there is the fear that you might not be able to return. I always vote for the things that I definitely want going in the first load. Anything after that is gravy. Our first load consisted of the French chairs Bill wanted and the dining room furniture that I wanted, plus a few added perks thrown in for fun.

We had already decided that the best thing would be to take everything to my condo since I had a garage. Once it was all safe and secure, we could conquer and divide the loot. I only had a one-car garage so we carefully stacked pieces where we could. Since it was clear the dining room furniture was mine, we went ahead and brought it inside. Bill and Dan's items, along with those yet to be determined, went into my garage.

"Ready to go back?" asked Bill.

"Not until I go to the bathroom," replied Dan. "I don't know what's up, but my stomach is a mess."

Bill and I both laughed, having been down this road before.

"Okay, now are we ready?" Bill asked once Dan reappeared.

"Yes, but the two of you need to wait in the van at the

church and let me circle the complex just to make sure nothing looks suspicious," I instructed.

It was already one in the morning when we got back. I rode by the unit and then circled the entire complex. I did not notice any additional cars and the office and clubhouse lights were the same as earlier. All of the condos were dark, either from their owners going to bed or not yet occupied. Just to be sure, I pulled into the drive in front of the garage and partially raised the door. It looked the same. I then went back to the church, waved to the boys and they followed me to our destination.

I let Bill back his van in and once again, I parked my car a couple of doors down in front of a vacant unit. He and Dan were already loading when I walked up. I hurried to help. Once the van was full, Bill went back to the church to wait while Dan helped me fill up my car. He then jumped in the front seat and squeezed my crotch.

"Having fun?" Dan said with a gleam in his eye.

"Yes, and don't distract me." I replied with a grin.

We made the trek back out to my condo and unloaded everything. There were four units in my building so I wanted to make sure that we were as quiet as possible. My garage was quickly filling up, but at least both vehicles were now empty. We came inside and sat down for a minute. I sat on one end of my sofa and Bill on the other. I thought Dan would go for a chair, but instead he sat down between us and rested a hand on Bill's leg and the other on mine.

"Are you as tired as I am?" I asked.

"More so. I catered a luncheon today. But we still have more to load," said Bill.

"Do we?" I asked. "There was only that club chair, one table, no, two tables left."

"There was a mirror that we did not bring down to the garage," said Dan, chiming in.

"Is it worth the risk?" I asked.

"It is always worth the risk," Bill said.

I really did not want to go back. I always preferred one or, at the most, two trips per heist ever since that time the police pulled Greg and me over on our third run. The risk gets greater with each return visit. Was there really enough left to take that chance?

"If you don't want to go, Dan and I can swing by on our way home," Bill said sensing my reservation.

That was all it took because I knew Bill was dead serious. Maybe there were some things that we had missed. After all, we had not looked through the boxes.

"Fine. Let's do this," I said as I hauled my tired ass off of the sofa.

The third run. This time my stomach was acting up from nerves. It was careless. It was foolish. *Why am I going? And more importantly, do I have any Kleenex?*

We did not bother checking things out first but simply headed straight to the unit. That is the problem with too many trips. You get cocky, careless. I knew better but did not say anything.

We quickly loaded the remaining pieces from the garage into Bill's van and then grabbed the mirror that Dan had mentioned. There was another lamp, nothing special but we thought *Why not?* I noticed that Bill had begun to open one of the packing boxes.

"No," I said. Bill just looked at me.

"If we are going to take the time to go through the boxes, then we don't need our cars out front and the garage door open," I added.

Again, careless, foolish. I could tell that he had not even thought of that.

"You are right. Let's go," said Bill.

We closed the van and the garage door. There had not even been enough left to use my car, so I drove it home empty. I wondered if Bill and Dan were planning on going back and sorting through the packing boxes. I hoped not. One, they might be filled with personal keepsakes. Two, it was risky and if they got caught, then I would be caught. I could not trust them not to sing loudly if taken into custody.

I don't know for sure if they did or did not go back but I never saw anything to indicate that they did.

Back at my condo, we unloaded the van. It was already after two in the morning.

"Do you want to divide everything now or get some sleep and do it tomorrow?" Bill asked. I hoped that they would want to wait.

"Let's wait. I am exhausted and my stomach still isn't right," Dan replied.

"Sounds good. Tomorrow it is," I added.

All of our schedules were flexible so we decided to get together mid-afternoon.

After a few hours of sleep, I felt somewhat refreshed. A long hot shower and light breakfast also helped. Dan and Bill arrived around two and I could tell that they felt better as well. I invited them in and offered each a soft drink. We sat for a few minutes to discuss just how the three of us were going to divide everything.

"I think that we should take turns," said Bill.

"I agree," I said.

"I wanted the pair of French chairs so that should be two turns," said Bill. "Or one for me and one for Dan. You wanted the dining table. One turn. The set of chairs. A very generous second turn."

"Okay," I agreed. It seemed fair enough—although I realized that with Dan and Bill both choosing separately that they were going to get two-thirds of the take. Still, they both worked hard for it and I really did not need or have room for much.

"Good," said Bill. "So, you took a turn, then me, then Dan and then you again. That takes care of what we called 'dibs' on. So that would mean it is my turn and I choose the bow-front chest."

Damn, I really wanted that. But fair is fair.

"Dan?"

"I have been thinking and I would like that rug, you know, the one with all the reds," said Dan."

Great, I couldn't use it. I was pleased by his choice.

"My turn?" I asked. "I'll take the antique lowboy." I could tell from Bill's expression that he had been hopeful that he would take it home. But he recovered and asked for the English chest.

"The pair of crystal lamps," said Dan. "I am assuming that would be considered as one, since your eight chairs were done that way."

Was he being sarcastic? Maybe not, but I did not want to say anything because they might come back with thinking that the pair of French chairs should count as one and not two turns.

"Great. I would like the mirror," I said quickly, before they had time to think about it.

"I want the club chair," followed Bill.

"The brass lamp with the black shade." And on and on it went, until everything was spoken for. I ended up with the dining room furniture and the burl-top lowboy with a gold leaf mirror to hang over it. I also got two rugs, two small tables, a lamp and a wooden box. There were a few more accessories I chose as we got down to the final pieces. The boys took home two-thirds of everything and the petty part of me thought that they would not have known about any of it, if not for me. Still, I could not have moved everything by myself and some is better than none.

Bill and Dan managed to get everything in one load, which surprised me. I asked if they needed me to come help them unload and move everything upstairs, but they said "No." That was a relief. I was in the mood to move, arrange and fluff my home with all the newly gathered antiques. The pieces made such a statement – one of which was, "Hey, I am very recognizable. Better not ever have this home photographed."

A local designer, who had worked for Palmer's Fine Furniture, had that happen. Over a period of a couple of years, pieces came up missing but no one at the store suspected the designer. However, once he left and went out on his own, he had the opportunity to have his home photographed for the newspaper. In the photos were some of the missing furniture and accessories. The store owners chose not to prosecute, but word quickly spread through the community and his reputation was toast.

There was always the fear that someone would be in our home and might know the person we had robbed. They could recognize a piece or two and let the victims know. However, as time moved on, it was easy not to think too much about it. Still, there was always that possibility hanging out there. Always that danger lurking.

Chapter Eleven

You know, someone did steal something from me once. Of course, it was something that I had stolen first – a pair of black garden urns on stands. I had them on each side of my front door for years. And then one morning I went out to pick up my newspaper and thought something wasn't quite right. It took just a moment before it sank in – the urns were gone. I was furious! *How dare anyone steal from me!* And then I realized the absolute absurdness of that feeling. I have said it before, karma really is a bitch.

I called Bill and Dan and told them what had happened.

"Really? We just added a pair of black urns on our terrace," Bill said while trying to keep his composure.

"Bitch. You did not," I said.

"Trust me, I know better than to steal from you. You would just steal it back," Bill said with a laugh.

"Probably true. Still, it irks me," I continued.

"It would me, too," Bill agreed.

"Anyway, how about dinner tonight? My treat," I offered.

"Sounds good," he replied. "We have been wanting to talk with you about something anyway."

Uh oh, surely they were not wanting to go back out on a midnight run this soon after our wonderful find of antiques. We made plans to meet at a nearby restaurant at six. I was curious all day as to what they might want to discuss but was pleasantly surprised when I learned that they wanted to go to the beach and hoped that I might like to join them.

Perfect.

"I would love to," I said sincerely.

We made plans to go in a couple of weeks and I decided to drive. I dreaded the long haul but agreed to do it, since we could make our destination in one day. We made reservations for adjoining rooms at a new motel right on the water.

Once we arrived I felt the stress of my design clients from hell leaving my body. I sat on the balcony and enjoyed the view. We also lay out on the beach, which left me sun-burned, although not quite as bad as I have been in the past. I'll have to say that Dan looked mighty tasty in his bathing suit but then Bill wasn't too shabby either. There were a few other guys of like mind staying at the motel, as well as some young families with cute daddies. Unfortunately, they had accessorized themselves with kids, which was an immediate buzzkill for me.

I did meet one guy at the swimming pool who kept pursuing me. He was very attractive but slightly inebriated and managed to stay that way the entire trip. However, that did not prevent me from letting him woo me all the way back to my room.

One day Bill, Dan and I rode around after lunch and saw a new subdivision with signage advertising furnished models.

"What do you think?" asked Bill.

"It can't hurt to look," I replied.

I pulled my car into a guest parking spot and we went in for a tour. The saleslady on duty thought she had hot prospects coming through the door and began her song and dance. I cut her off and asked if she wouldn't mind if we just had a look.

"Of course, make yourself at home. I have brochures on that table over there," she offered.

"Thank you," said Bill.

The model was a one-level number with a screen-enclosed swimming pool. The furnishings were very "beachy." Perfect for that house and location, but not anything we would want to risk trying to pilfer. However, there were a couple of festive accessories that might have made nice gifts. Still, with the agent at her desk, I shook my head from side to side when Dan picked up a fish sculpture and looked at me longingly.

"No," I said sternly.

There were two other homes open, but neither had furnishings. Still, we enjoyed seeing them and talked about what we might do if we owned them.

"I cannot imagine having a beach house. How decadent it would feel just to be able to swim naked in the pool!" said Bill.

I let my mind wander at that comment thinking that I would not mind watching or participating.

"I unlocked a window," Dan said after we were back in the car.

"Why?" I asked staring at him.

"I want that fish," he answered.

"It is not worth the risk. We may have been the only people there today. It would be easy to remember three queens prancing through, sprinkling fairy dust on everything," I explained.

"I resemble that remark," said Bill.

"Yes, you do, sweetie. Yes, you do," I chuckled.

I could tell Dan was disappointed. Sometimes he acted just like a child. However, I do know for a fact that in bed he was all man.

"What are you smiling at?" Bill asked looking at me.

"Nothing. Just having fun," I replied.

Later that evening, I got together with my intoxicated friend and ordered room service. I let Bill and Dan have my car so that they could go out to eat. I did not think about the beach house again until the next morning, when I opened the door connecting our rooms and saw the fish sculpture sitting on their TV.

"What the hell?" was all that I said.

I was speechless. Well, actually, not speechless but I was afraid that if I said what I thought that it might end a friendship or two. I closed the door, locked it from my side and immediately realized my mistake because they still had my car keys.

Mr. Slurred Speech had a name and that name was Leon. I woke him and said it was time to shower. He was hungover but after four days of being with him, I knew that this was his usual state. To keep him moving, I got in the shower with him. He was feeling frisky and while that was tempting, I just wanted to get dressed and away before Bill and Dan tried to explain, or apologize, or even say "Hello."

I heard one of them try the connecting door and then knock softly. I ignored it and they did not try again. Leon and I got dressed and headed to the motel restaurant to grab coffee and breakfast. I think this was the first time that the two of us had a sober conversation and I kind of liked it. He was an adorable drunk, but even more adorable when he had his wits about him. It turned out that we had quite a bit in common in our likes and dislikes.

But at the moment I was still focused on my present dislike of Bill and Dan.

"What's up with you and your friends?" Leon asked. "It is like you wanted to get away from them."

"Just a little disagreement. I had asked them not to do something but they went ahead and did it anyway," I replied.

"Now don't get me wrong, or think that I am taking sides, but why did you think they would do what you asked?

Do they always listen to you?" Leon inquired.

"No, rarely," I answered with a laugh.

"So, why now?" he wanted to know.

"Because it was something risky and unnecessary," I replied.

"What? Were they trying to kill someone? Steal something? What?" Leon asked.

I don't know what possessed me to be truthful. I said, "Steal" and then went on to explain what had happened.

Leon asked if I was mad at the fact that they did it, or mad because they did without me – or that they used my car.

"Yes, to all of the above," I answered.

"Then let's go steal something for ourselves," he suggested.

"What?" I asked in disbelief.

"We should go steal something," repeated Leon.

I did not know whether to be excited or scared. I opted for a little of both. My mind was racing as I tried to decide how I should respond. Do I agree? Act eager? Act offended? I decided to play along and find out what he had in mind.

"Let's go back to the same place that they hit and get something for ourselves," he suggested.

"Way too risky. The three of us were just there yesterday," I said. "I think the realtor might remember me and I can't even be sure that the fish sculpture was the only thing that they took."

"Then let's find our own spot. There are new developments going up all over town with models," said Leon. "Care to ride around?"

"They have my car keys," I replied.

"I have a car," said Leon.

Good to know. I had only seen Leon by the pool or in my bed. I did not think about him driving. But I did not want to think about him driving drunk.

"Let's go," I said since Leon was currently sober.

We spent the entire day together without a drop of alcohol. I realized that I felt more than just a sexual attraction to him. Of course it did not hurt that he was adorable, blonde and had a sexy tan line. I felt relaxed and was actually enjoying myself. He was charming, funny and constantly horny. I had hit the trifecta. It also made me smile when I thought that Bill and Dan were probably wondering where I was and maybe, just maybe, they were a little bit concerned. After all, we were supposed to be headed home the next morning.

Leon and I walked through several model homes before the day ended. He managed to charm all of the saleswomen and I think at least one salesman with his easy demeanor. I saw several things that I would not have minded pocketing, so we left windows unlocked at three different homes.

Now granted, I would have been fine to not follow through, but it seemed important to Leon that we had something to show for all of our efforts.

I had noticed at one of the earlier places we visited that their hours posted were 10 – 4. It was now 4:45. I mentioned that to Leon and described which one. I was glad that he remembered it and how to get back there. We pulled into their guest parking lot around five, got out of his car and proceeded to walk around as we checked out our surroundings. It was a three-story beachfront condo building with entrances near an exterior walkway and not an interior hall. The model/office was on the ground level and the window was still unlocked. (I know that if I was ever put in the situation of watching over or being responsible for a furnished model, I would make sure to check the windows each night before closing up.)

The condo's layout was designed with a couple of windows on the parking lot side and sliding glass doors across the back, looking out over the spectacular view. Because there were units sharing a common wall on each side, we had no other option but to raise the front window and crawl through. When it appeared that no one was out and about, I did just that and then went around to open the front door for Leon.

We had decided earlier that we did not need anything big. Just a little souvenir of our time together. There were several nautical-themed gewgaws sitting around on tables and bathroom vanities to choose from. Leon looked at me strangely when I said that word.

"It means useless, worthless trinkets," I explained.

"Oh, that pretty much sums it up. Still, which one do you want?" he asked.

I opened the cabinet under the kitchen sink and found a trash can with a plastic bag liner. I did not see any more bags so I tossed the couple of wadded up paper towels it held and brought the bag over to Leon. He had picked out a wooden lighthouse and I grabbed a fake conch shell. We put them in the plastic bag so that it would look like we were taking out the trash when we left. I surveyed the parking lot from the front window just to make sure the coast was clear and spotted a car driving through the entrance. It appeared to be headed for a parking space in front. I had no idea if they lived there or worked there, but I knew that we did not need to be in the model if someone started to unlock the door.

"Out the back. Now!" I yelled to Leon.

He unlocked the sliding glass door and we stepped out onto the patio. I pulled the door closed but had no way to lock it back. We walked around the building and headed for the spot where he had parked his car. I peeked out from the corner of the building and saw that the car had in fact parked in front of the model unit. It was the saleslady and I watched as she unlocked the door and went inside.

"She must have forgotten something," said Leon.

"I doubt that she will notice the two missing treasures. Unless someone saw me going through the window and alerted her," I added.

I was grateful that our car was not directly in front of the model and that we did not have to pass the unit to retrieve it. We jumped in and I put the bag in the backseat. Leon started the engine and was backing out just as she exited the unit. I hid my face with my hand but watched through my fingers. She barely glanced our way.

"I don't think she suspected anything," said Leon.

"Do realize how close that was? What if she had come in while we were still there?" I said.

"Ménage à trois?" Leon said with a sexy smile.

We both laughed nervously, but neither one of us felt at ease until we were further away from the complex.

"Where to?" he asked.

"Dinner and then bed," I instructed.

"Yes, sir," he confirmed.

We both wanted to freshen up before dinner and each went back to our motel rooms. Clearly Bill and Dan heard me come in because they immediately knocked on the door that connected our rooms. This time I decided to open it.

"Where have you been? You have had us worried half to death," Bill asked.

"And you don't think that I was worried after I realized you had gone out on a midnight run?" I countered.

"Technically it was more like eleven-thirty," Bill replied.

I just glared. "Really, you want to take the smart-ass approach with me right now, Bill?" I challenged.

Dan immediately started apologizing and saying it was all his fault and that they had just thought it would be fun. He added that they had actually picked up the fish for me.

"No, you didn't," I said, looking Dan in the eyes.

"You're right," he said looking away.

"I told you that he wouldn't fall for it," Bill said.

"It's fine. Just caught me off guard," I said before continuing. "I have got to get cleaned up and meet Leon for dinner. Want to join us?"

"Leon? The lush has a name?" asked Bill.

"Yes, and I have spent the day with him and really like him. So don't be bitchy," I answered.

Now that the latest drama was settled, I jumped in the shower, fluffed my hair and changed clothes. Oops, maybe I was premature in thinking that it was settled. I remembered that Bill and Dan still did not know about my day. I was sure that they would react every bit as badly as I did.

Leon knocked on my door, looking very handsome in seersucker and linen. He gave me a long kiss and I could taste liquor. That's fine. After the day that we had, a cocktail seemed in order.

"Bill and Dan want to join us. Is that okay?" I asked.

"Sure, something tells me that I am going to be seeing a lot of them," answered Leon.

What did that mean? Is he planning to come for a visit? How do I feel about that? You know, I think I like it.

The four of us piled into my car and headed for a seafood restaurant we had been told was one of the best in the area. Bill kept asking Leon questions, which I thought on one hand was rude – but on the other hand, I was enjoying getting to learn a little more about him. Leon was being a good sport and even asked a few questions of his own. Bill was slightly guarded with his answers but Dan was like an open book. Still, watching Dan pull out his flirtatious charm had me saying under my breath, "He's mine, Bitch. Step back."

"Did you say something?" asked Leon.

"No," I said shaking my head.

The food was wonderful and worthy of the praise it had been given. I had one drink. Bill and Dan had two each, but Leon was now on his fourth. *Clearly this is a problem. How do I feel about it? Not sure.* The conversation was easy and light now that Bill had gotten his questionnaire out of the way.

"You never did say what the two of you were up to all day," said Dan.

"We rode around checking everything out," I replied.

"Yeah, we looked at a bunch of furnished models," said Leon, feeling free and loose with his tongue.

Bill's eyebrows raised and I braced myself for what was about to happen.

"Did you find anything interesting?" Bill asked.

"Oh yeah, lots," Leon continued. He then turned to me and asked "Didn't you show them what we picked up?"

Oh, shit.

Bill and Dan were at full attention.

"Picked up? What did you pick up?" Bill asked.

"We decided that since you went shopping last night, we would do the same," I stated.

"We?" asked Bill.

"We?" asked Dan.

"Yes, we. Leon knew that I was upset with the two of you so I explained to him why. And he wanted to cheer me up. And let's just say that he did a really good job," I replied.

At this point it could have gone either way. The boys could have jumped up in a huff but instead Bill started laughing. Then Dan. Then Leon and finally I succumbed to the laughter and joined in.

"Well, it appears we have a foursome," said Bill.

I thought, *No. A quintet.* I missed Greg and wondered if he was okay and if he was happy to be back in his hometown.

Leon and I had that last night together and then we exchanged our phone numbers and parted. I found that I had really become attached to him in that short period of time. But then, I have always jumped in with both feet when anyone paid attention to me.

The drive home felt like it took forever. There was a part of me that was anxious to get back just so I could call Leon and make sure that he had given me a real phone number. I had been fooled before.

"Are we going to see Leon again?" asked Bill.

"I hope so," I replied.

"I liked him," added Dan.

"Me, too," I agreed.

After that, Leon and I talked often and made plans to meet a distance halfway between us one weekend. I was nervous. *Would it be like before? Better? Not as good?* We were together Friday night through Sunday afternoon. Most of the time was spent in our motel room until we finally both got a little stir crazy and decided to go for a ride.

"Do you want to go shopping?" I asked.

"Shopping or SHOPPING?" Leon replied.

"No, legitimate shopping. We don't know our way around here and it would be way too dangerous to try anything else," I offered.

"That's fine. I am good either way," he said.

Leon stayed sober – well, fairly sober most of the weekend. Saturday night we went to a gay bar and he did get a little tipsy. But I will say this for him, he stayed by my side and rebuked anyone who tried to get his attention. A perfect gentleman until we got back to our room and the clothes came off.

"I have had such a good time being with you," I said.

"Same here," he added sweetly.

"I don't want to go," I blurted. *Uh oh... was I getting too needy too soon?*

"Why don't I come to visit you next time instead of you having to meet me halfway?" offered Leon.

"I would like that," I said.

We pulled out of the motel parking lot together but in separate cars, headed in different directions. It was a long and lonely trip home. However, Bill and Dan were waiting for me when I got back and wanted all of the details.

"Spill," said Dan.

"It was good, I mean really good. He is coming here next time," I confided.

"You did not go on a midnight run, did you?" Bill asked.

"No."

"You swear?" added Dan.

"Yes, I swear."

I decided that there was no sense in telling them that the subject did come up. They probably did not believe me and thought that I had masterminded a job or two while I was away – little did they know, we rarely even got out of bed.

"What about the two of you? Did you get into any trouble?" I inquired.

"Without you? Never!" said Bill. Somehow I did not fully believe him.

"Well, if he does come to town and you want to find a little something for us to check out, we are in," said Bill while Dan shook his head in agreement.

"Let's just play it by ear," I said.

Chapter Twelve
present day

The first day of my two-day moving sale was about to come to an end. By all accounts, it was successful. The folks helping me were saying things like "It is the biggest sale we have ever held." Or "We have never had a sale with this much high quality furniture and accessories."

"Did Palmer's Furniture go out of business once you stopped buying?" asked Roberta Ann. "It is like you had your own branch of the store. I recognize all of their high-end brands so don't try to deny it."

If truth be told, I am sure my inventory put a serious dent in their business. At one time, I tried to add up everything Nathaniel and the Midnight Movers had stolen from them. I wished that I had kept a running inventory through the years. It would have been interesting. I know for a fact that there were five condominium models from three different complexes. And then there was the model at the home tour years ago. That was one of our biggest heists ever and I heard that it was the one that about did them in – or at least, it caused them to no longer furnish houses or models. I am sure that they had insurance to help with their loses but with just the thefts that we were responsible for, I imagine that their insurance premiums skyrocketed or maybe their company dropped them leaving their agent scrambling for another option.

I did not have a personal vendetta against the store or the owners. In fact, they had been good to my family and me over the years. I often would bring my design clients by and had even made some legitimate purchases.

The only bad experience I had was when the daughter inherited the store and her husband helped her to run it. I was fresh out of college and eager to learn more about design and I applied for a job there selling furniture. The jerk of a husband interviewed me but cut it very short. Either he was having a really bad day or he was truly an asshole. Regardless he looked at me and asked, "Why should hire you? What makes you think I'd want someone as inexperienced as you on my payroll? You don't have anything to offer me. You're just wasting my time as well as yours, but I doubt that you have anything better to do."

I remembered being stunned as I looked at him in disbelief. Surely he was joking, though it was not the least bit funny. Cruel would be a better way to describe his tirade. I waited for a second thinking he would apologize. But no, he just stared back and then finally said "Go on, get out. There is no place for you at Palmer's."

"What did you ask? Oh, yeah, you are right. You got me. I did love that store and was sorry to see it close," I replied, adding: "But I certainly will not miss the Palmer daughter's husband."

Roberta Ann's sweet expression immediately changed.

"Oh, he was a real son of a biscuit-eater, wasn't he?"

I was shocked. She knew him, too.

"The only joy that I got by them going out of business was knowing that jerk would be unemployed," she added.

"You are preaching to the choir, sister. I could not stand that man and almost did not want to take my clients in there because of his two-faced demeanor. What did he do to you?" I asked.

"He was so ugly to my parents. Well, really to my daddy. He had sweet-talked my mother into thinking she needed a complete dining room suite. But she really did not have room for the buffet, just the table, chairs and server. Still he kept charming her until she finally said she guessed that she would take it. My daddy stood up and looked him in the eye and said 'No sir, we do not need it. Appreciate your help but I am going to have to say no.' With that, the asshole turned on them with such venom that my mother started crying and my dad said that they were leaving. Then the prick followed them to the door and said 'Good riddance.' I mean, what a schmuck! My mother wanted that furniture so badly but no one else in town carried that brand."

I could not help myself. I started laughing and apologized for doing so.

"I am so sorry," I said. Well, she started laughing, too, and then we had a name war trying to think of things to call him.

"He was a bastard," began Roberta Ann.

"A jackass," I added.

"Asswipe," Roberta Ann said surprising me.

"S.O.B.," I continued.

"Motherf..." Roberta Ann quickly covered her mouth muffling the word. "Oops, I did not mean to go that far. But any time I think about him, I still get angry and my parents have been dead and gone for years. Hopefully he is, too."

How refreshing it was to be able to vent with someone. I decided that the more I got to know Roberta Ann, the more that I liked her.

"I hope tomorrow will be a good day too. I promise to try and hold my tongue," I said.

"Don't bother on my account. Some of these fools need a good slap across the face, verbally speaking. And I think, Ricky, that you are just the man to do it," she said.

"Yes, I am. The joys of being old."

"Something tells me that you have always been this way," she said with a grin.

"Guilty."

I mean, how could I argue with that?

Chapter Thirteen

True to his word, Leon did come to town for a weekend visit. I was anxious to show him off and decided to host a party. Bill and Dan helped me gather and prepare the food as well as the guest list. And while I had lots of acquaintances, Bill and Dan had become my closest friends since Greg moved away and Dean fell in love again.

I invited thirty people but closer to fifty showed up. I should have put on the invitation that guests of guests may not invite guests. I kept introducing myself to strangers and asking, "Who did you come with?" There were a couple of guys who told me the name of their dates and I had to reply, "I don't know who that is." One guy told me that he was a friend of the host. I looked at him and said, "Really, I'm the host."

"No, you're not," said the snippy prima donna, and then proceeded to point out the one who he thought was giving the party.

Regardless, it was fun and I think Leon had a good time, as well as Bill and Dan. I was grateful that they also helped watch and made sure the nosey queens did not go through my drawers or pocket any small items. We were all very familiar with thieves so we knew what to look out for. My home managed to come out unscathed with the exception of a few spilled drinks.

"I think that I would like to move here," said Leon after we fell into bed exhausted.

I figured that it was the alcohol talking but the next morning he reaffirmed his desire to move in with me if I would have him. *A couple. I was about to become part of "A couple."*

"Yes, please. I would like that very much," I said sincerely. We had made plans to join Bill and Dan for Sunday brunch before Leon hit the road and headed home. Needless to say, they were a bit surprised by the news.

"Kind of sudden, isn't it?" asked Bill.

"I am happy for you both. We are going to have so much fun together," said Dan, offering a much more positive response.

I must admit that as excited as I felt, I still had a bit of apprehension. *Am I ready to have Leon around full-time? Do I really know him all that well?*

But then I thought: when we do another midnight run with Bill and Dan, then we would get half and they would get half instead of me getting just a third. *Wait a second, am I making a relationship decision based on getting more goods from the next robbery? And, will there even be a next robbery?*

After Leon hit the road, I called Greg. I had not spoken with him in a while and although I had told him about Leon, he was unaware at how serious things had gotten.

"Hey, old friend. How ya doing?" I greeted Greg when he answered.

"I am so glad that you called, I have big news," he replied. *Great. Greg has big news and I have big news. So whose news is bigger?*

"I am moving back to town and wondered if I could stay with you until I get my feet on the ground," he asked.

"Really? That makes me so happy," I said excitedly. "What brought this on?"

"I miss the big city and my family here is driving me crazy," he replied. "I've been sending out my resume and just got a job offer back at the bank."

"That's great and of course, you can stay with me for a while," I told him.

"Thanks, now what's your news?" he asked.

"Leon is moving in with me," I told him.

Dead silence.

"Greg, you still there?" I asked.

"It's kind of sudden, isn't it? I mean, what has it been, six months?" he said.

"Just a little over six," I said defensively.

Greg then went on to tell me that he was happy for me but I sensed he was also jealous. He and I had never been romantic but always had a loving friendship. Even though we both dated other people, nothing ever seemed serious for either of us – even my few months with Bill (and his family) had seemed destined to fail from the start. I was not sure if Greg was upset that I had found someone or that things would be different when he moved back. Bill had Dan and now I had Leon. Greg was still single and I knew all too well just how it felt to be single around couples.

"Listen, I am really happy for you but I will need to find somewhere else to stay. You don't need me around while you are trying to set up housekeeping with Leon," Greg said. "Anyway, I can't wait to see you and look forward to meeting your other half."

We talked a while longer but it felt a little awkward. I really was thrilled that Greg was moving back and hoped that he and Leon would not see each other as competitors fighting for my attention. I wanted us all to get along. I was also smart enough to know that a lot of that depended on me. I had to make sure neither one of them ever felt that I was taking sides.

—•—

I ran by Bill and Dan's apartment to tell them the news. We fixed cocktails and found our seats in their beautiful living room. Bill and Dan chose the French chairs from our most recent run and I took my place on the sofa. You know, the faux-suede one that Greg and I had managed to get away with, in spite of Bill's car breaking down.

"Well, this could get complicated," grumbled Bill.

"Why do you say that, Bill? Greg is my oldest friend. He is happy for me and I am happy to have him back in town. I think that he and Leon will really get along," I said hopefully.

"If you say so," said Bill.

"I can't wait to have Greg back," added Dan, realizing that he needed to step in. "He's a stitch and I am wild about Leon. It is going to be wonderful. Can you imagine the damage we could do? I mean, think of how big of a job we could pull off with 5 guys."

"And think of how much more risky it would be," I said. "Five guys keeping their mouths shut. Five guys fighting over stolen goods. Five guys..."

"Yeah, I get it," Dan said, waving his hand in surrender. "But I don't think that it is impossible. When will Greg be back?"

"His job doesn't start for another six weeks. He's planning on moving back next month. I offered for him to stay with me. But with all of his furniture and stuff, he would have to store it and then move it again when he found his own place. So he is thinking that he will just go ahead and get an apartment now," I informed them.

"And Leon?" Bill asked.

"He is moving next week. I am glad that he will have a few weeks to get acclimated before Greg hits town. I am still trying to find him a clerical job. That's what he is doing now and he seems to enjoy it," I said.

Bill asked if I had a copy of Leon's resume and offered to help through his connections. I told him that I did but then I had to level with him. There is a bit of a problem in his time line – like a three-year lapse between jobs.

"How did he explain it?" Bill asked.

"At first he said he took three years off to travel, but the more we talked about it, things just weren't adding up," I confided.

"And the real reason?" Bill asked.

"I pressed him and then he came clean. He was in prison. It was a white-collar crime. Embezzling," I said hesitantly.

"Shit," Bill and Dan said in unison.

I could not argue with that. It was a big load of crap to deal with and I was not sure if he could still get a job, especially if it dealt with numbers and money.

"Leon stole money. We steal furniture," said Dan. "What's the difference, other than he got caught? We are all thieves and it is just by dumb luck that we have gotten away with everything so far."

"True," I nodded.

I really did appreciate the fact that I had bared my soul and shared Leon's secret and that they understood and did not appear to think any less of him. We have all made mistakes and probably will continue to unless we change our evil ways. Speaking of which...

"I think there might be a midnight run coming up. Interested?" I asked.

—●—

Leon arrived with all of his earthly possessions in the back of his car. Other than closet and drawer space, I did not have to move much around to make room. He did have an oil painting that I thought was about the most hideous thing that I had ever seen. Supposedly it had some significance to his childhood. I was ready to say it was not going in our home until he pointed out that he had painted it while in high school and actually won some kind of an award. I wondered if it was like those kids' sporting events where everyone gets a trophy just for showing up. There was no way that I could express my true thoughts without hurting him.

"I will find just the perfect spot for it... later," I said. And thought to myself: *much, much later.*

Bill and Dan came by the condo to welcome Leon to town and Dan immediately spotted the painting.

"What the f...?" Dan said as I quickly cut him off.

"Isn't it great? Leon painted it in high school and won an award," I cheerfully explained.

By then, Bill had turned his attention toward the chaos on canvas sitting on the floor.

"You better get that on the wall," Bill said sarcastically. "You wouldn't want something to happen to it."

I glared at Bill and he responded in kind but Leon seemed oblivious.

"Thanks, Bill," said Leon as he lifted the painting up, set it on top of the antique lowboy and leaned it against the elegant gold leaf mirror hanging on the wall.

"Much better," Bill dared to say, garnering him a second intense glare from me.

Dan decided to change the subject as he took a seat.

"So, have you found out any more about the home tour?" he asked.

"What home tour?" Leon asked with interest.

"Well, every year a bunch of builders get together and they each build a new home side by side and then open them to the public for a tour," I explained as I sat down on the sofa. "They go into a new subdivision where they can have adjoining lots on a cul-de-sac. That makes it easier for folks to view the houses. They can park and simply walk door to door."

"And this is coming up soon?" asked Leon as he and Bill found chairs.

"Yes, they are already advertising the dates. It opens in less than three weeks," I said.

Leon was excited, but since he had never attended anything like this before, he was also concerned. And rightly so.

"Are they furnished? And if so, wouldn't there be security of some sort?" Leon asked.

"Yes, and yes," I replied.

"But Ricky has a plan and is checking daily," added Bill.

"You see, what usually happens is one house gets ready way ahead of the others. They get it all decorated and such and then have it photographed. That way the newspaper and whatever media they are using can start promoting with photos." I had everyone's attention now. "I keep checking on the progress and it appears to me that there are two homes nearing completion. The other builders will probably be finishing their homes on the day it opens. And there is one that I doubt will even be ready by the time the tour concludes."

I explained further that it would be crazy busy around there in the daytime with all of the builders and subs rushing to get finished – but at night it would be like a ghost town.

"And there doesn't appear to be any security yet. I am hoping that they wait for that until everything is finished and decorated," I added.

"I keep going by there to check because any day now, I am sure one of those houses will get a shitload of furniture delivered and be set up for photos. I am hoping that they will wait until all of the houses are finished before bringing in the security. Of course, right now the local cops might do a drive by every now and then," I added.

"And you think this is safe?" Leon asked. "You think that we can pull it off and not get caught?"

Making eye contact with each of them, I answered.

"There is a risk of getting caught anytime we do a job, even if it is just for a fish sculpture or a fake conch shell. That is why I am doing all that I can to plan and prepare us for it," I said.

Bill was listening intently to everything and realized something that might be a problem.

"You said the houses are all on a cul-de-sac, right?" Bill asked. "That means dead end, right? Which means we would be trapped if anyone blocked the road?"

"Yes, but there are no houses backing up to one side. It is just a big field and then a road and then another field. I am thinking that we should park on the far street and walk through the field and then come in from the back," I continued. "Then we will do like always and gather everything before moving your van and my car."

"Should we take all of our cars?" asked Dan.

"I don't think so. One, it might look strange having three cars and a van parked on that road at night," I answered. "Plus, I think it would just add to the risk of one of us getting caught. You know, a taillight out, going too fast, too slow, driving erratically – anything that might cause one of us to be pulled over. There is always the chance of that happening with two vehicles but the risk doubles if we each have a car."

"I agree," said Leon adding his support. "Two cars and maybe no more than two trips."

"Or one trip and four cars," Dan said after seeing the flaw in Leon's comment.

This was going nowhere so I suggested that we table it for now. I was not even 100% sure that it would really happen. It all depended on when the first house was ready and what the builders did about security at that point. I told them to just let me keep checking and then we would decide. But we would need to be ready to move as soon as the furnishings went in. I felt there would be a very short window of opportunity.

"We have a banquet to cater this Thursday but other than that, our nights are free. And even that should be over and cleared away by eleven," said Bill.

When Bill said "We," he meant Dan and himself. Bill needed help and Dan needed a job so they were now working together. I think Bill's father even helped sometimes. I had asked Dan one time how he got along with his father-in-law and he replied with clenched teeth "Peachy, just peachy." He did not have to say anything more as I felt his pain.

Every day I would ride through the subdivision to check on progress. There was so much activity that I could not actually drive onto the street where the houses were being built. Trucks and cars lined the cul-de-sac and filled each of the homes' driveways. Everyone was rushing to be complete by the deadline. Some days I took my car and other days I would swap out for Leon's 1979 Plymouth Volare. I thought that might shake it up just a bit and not be as obvious.

Leon had been going on job interviews and helping Bill sometimes with the grunt work in his catering business. Finally he had a callback for a clerical job with one of the religious publishing houses. I prayed that they did not look into or would overlook the three-year lapse on his resume. Money was beginning to be tight in our household. I did not have a steady income being self-employed and some design clients were a little squirrelly and slow to pay when they received their invoices.

"I got the job," Leon said, finally.

Those four words made my day. I was afraid that if he stayed unemployed much longer that it really would put a strain on our relationship. He did not like being dependent on me and I was beginning to resent it myself, although I tried my best to hide it.

"I am so glad. When do you begin?" I asked joyfully.

"I start Monday but it will be two weeks before my first paycheck," he replied.

"That's okay. We're fine. I just hope that you will enjoy the job, or as well as anyone enjoys their job," I said encouragingly.

"It will be great. I will make sure of it," Leon said with a smile.

"Why don't we go out to dinner and celebrate? Then we can ride by the tour site and see if anything is happening," I offered.

We decided to go to our favorite Mexican restaurant. I truly thought that we both could live off guacamole, queso and chips. Of course, washing them down with Margaritas is an added bonus. In fact, we were so full by the time our dinner order arrived that we asked for a couple of to-go boxes to bring most of it home.

"You up for riding by the tour site?" I asked him.

"What do you think?" Leon replied with a slightly intoxicated smile.

I headed my car north from town in the direction of the tour subdivision. It was now dark and I assumed, like the nights before, all construction would be done until the next morning. Driving by in the evening had allowed me to actually go down the street and get a closer look as to which house might be the first completed. It appeared that it would be a toss up between one on the left and one of the ones on the right side of the cul-de-sac. I was hoping for the right simply because it backed up to the empty field.

These nightly drive-bys also gave me the opportunity to see if there was any security detail in place. One evening I did see a patrol car leaving the subdivision as I turned in. I do not know for sure if it was there because of the construction but it would make sense that they would ride by on occasion.

I turned right, then left, then right again into the cul-de-sac. I immediately stopped as soon as I realized that the large two-story home on the right had three furniture trucks in front.

Two men were carrying in a sofa while another man had a lamp in each hand.

"It's happening." I said thrilled and excited. Then I spotted the store logo on the side of the truck.

"Look, it's Palmer's. Well, at least we know it will be the good stuff," I added.

I pulled onto the shoulder of the road and managed a U-turn. I did not want to be seen scouting out the house. Leon turned around in his seat to see and I watched through my rearview mirror as I slowly drove us out of there.

"My stomach feels queasy. It must be the Mexican," Leon moaned.

"No sweetie, it's the midnight run nerves kicking in. I have some Kleenex in the glove box if you need me to pull over," I offered.

Leon said he would be okay until we got home.

"We need to call Bill and Dan," he added.

"No, we need to just go on by there," I confirmed.

—●—

Bill and Dan were not home. Where could they be? And then it sank in. It was Thursday — they said they had a catering job — a banquet. I decided to leave a note on their door asking them to call as soon as they got home, no matter how late. And I signed it "Nathaniel."

Neither Leon nor I were the least bit sleepy as we waited for their call. Finally around 11:30 the phone rang. I quickly picked up the receiver and said "Hello."

"What's up?" asked Bill.

"It's time," I said.

"Tonight?" he asked in anticipation.

"No, probably tomorrow night. You want to come over and discuss?" I asked hoping that they would.

"We are on our way," said Bill.

It was midnight when Bill and Dan rang our doorbell. Leon and I had been anxiously waiting for them to arrive.

"Come in. You want anything?" I offered.

They both said that they were fine as they each found a chair and sat down.

"Start talking," said Bill.

I explained how we went by after dinner and that they had three trucks unloading. I had thought about it and decided that as late as it was, most likely they were just dropping off. The store designers would be placing everything and hanging art and draperies tomorrow and maybe even the next day. I did not think that they could get everything in and finished in time to have it photographed for the Sunday paper. After all, this was already Thursday.

"I bet that they could," said Leon. "Time is running out and I doubt that they would photograph every room. Usually the paper only has two or three photos in an article, so they could just finish a few areas, have them photographed, and then take their time finishing everything else."

Bill agreed and I had to say, Leon made a valid point. *Look at my honey, all sober and making sense.* I was so proud.

"Fine, but what does that mean for us?" asked Dan.

"I think that it means tomorrow night might be best. The only unknown is the security. But I am afraid that if we wait much longer that there will be more homes completed and a greater need to add security," I said.

"More homes mean more options," added Bill.

"Right, but they had three trucks unloading and who knows, there could have been four or five truckloads altogether," I replied. "We will be doing good just to hit one house. Neither of us has that much extra room to store what we can't use. It's a big house, at least 4,000 square feet. Even if we get away with half of the loot, that's a lot."

"I'm with Ricky," said Dan turning to Bill. "Don't get greedy. I don't know where you think we are going to put whatever we find anyway."

"We are not always going to live in that apartment. I am hoping that we can buy a house one day," Bill replied.

"We have the same problem with space," I said. "I don't mind getting a storage unit until we are able to buy a bigger house, but damn, Leon just got a job. It may be a while."

"Leon got a job?" asked Bill. "Where?"

We took a few moments to bring them up to speed. Leon now had a 9:00 to 5:00 clerical job. Dan and Bill worked sporadic hours with their catering business and I was still juggling design clients. Some days were crazy busy and other days, I wondered if I would ever work again.

But for the last several months, business had been good. And now, Leon had a steady paycheck. We just might be able to buy a bigger place, too.

Dan gave Leon a hug that lasted a little longer than I thought that it should.

"So, what is our plan Ricky, I mean, Nathaniel?" Bill asked with a big silly grin on his face.

Chapter Fourteen

I swear it felt like Friday night would never arrive, but it finally did. I had been nervous all day. This was going to be huge. Huge risks and huge rewards.

The unknown factor was still the security issue. What if it had changed now that there was furniture in the house? How often would the police come by? And crap, what if the house had an alarm system? I can't believe that I was just now thinking of that. I did not want to get the others worked up so I chose not to say anything, other than that they needed to be prepared to walk away if it looked too risky. They agreed in theory but I knew that each one of them was thinking "Hell, no."

The four of us waited until ten to pull off the side of the road. I had been concerned about the van and my car sitting there. One vehicle on the side of the road might make you think car trouble. Two abandoned vehicles might make you think trouble, period. I convinced Bill to park his van at a nearby church lot since it had worked before. Then, with the four of us piled into my car, we headed down the dark deserted road where I pulled off onto the shoulder. There were no streetlights or houses in sight unless you counted the construction homes across the field.

"You are not going to believe this, but I have got to go to the bathroom and I am not talking number one," said Dan.

"I think I do too," chimed Bill.

"Aw hell, me too," said Leon.

Anticipating that this might happen, I reached under my seat and pulled out a roll of toilet paper.

"I came prepared. Tear off some sheets and head to the field," I instructed.

It was the most ridiculous thing, but all four of us had to take a squat in the field before we could go any further. Damn those *Midnight Run* runs.

"I hope that they can't track us by the deposits that we just left," Bill said once we were done and had come back together and started walking.

"Shh!" I said as Dan started laughing. All four of us had to put our hands over our mouths to muffle the giggles. Yeah, we were some kind of professionals weren't we? They never show that in a movie.

We managed to compose ourselves as we got closer to the house. A couple of lights had been left on inside but the neighboring homes were pitch black. I asked the three boys to stay in back as I cautiously went around to the front to see if anything appeared to be out of the norm. Fortunately, I did not see any cars or signs of security. We still did not know about the inside but that was a chance we were willing to take.

The exterior doors were locked, along with the garage doors. The windows were also locked and I did not find a key hidden in any of the obvious places. It was a two-story house but we were without a ladder. We had no way of knowing if any of the upstairs windows had been left unlocked anyway. None of us were anxious to bust down the door. The night was so peaceful that I feared the sound of breaking the door or even a window would echo for miles.

We had circled the house twice when Leon pointed upward to a plywood panel.

"What's that?" he asked.

The house was wood siding and in the dark the plywood had blended in, so I had missed it earlier.

"It looks like it is covering a window, or what is going to be a window," I said.

It was on the first floor but still high. I realized from the windows that I could see into, that we were standing outside of the master bedroom. And I was willing to bet that we were looking at a high window over a tub or something in the adjoining bath.

"If you can boost me up, I will see if I can pull the plywood off and crawl through," offered Dan.

Bill and Leon began to raise Dan up high enough to reach the bottom half of the plywood. It was nailed up there but not securely.

"Hold me," said Dan looking down. "I am going to try to pry it loose." He gave a tug and I saw movement. He tried again and I saw light peeking through. One more time and the plywood now appeared to be hanging by just one nail.

"Ricky, do you think that you can help catch it, if I give it another yank?" asked Dan.

"Whatever you do, make it quick," pleaded Bill. "I don't think that I can hold you much longer."

"Yes, I'm ready," I replied.

With that, Dan gave one more pull and I could see it coming loose. I was not sure that I could catch it but I wanted to at least keep it from hitting Leon or Bill in the head. I swatted at it and sent it off to the side causing it to hit the house. It made a bit of a thump but not too loud. With that, Dan hoisted himself inside and we all heard a thud.

"Are you okay?" asked Bill.

"Yes, I fell into the tub," replied Dan from inside. "I will go around back and open it up."

I did not hear an alarm and I thought that most likely it did not have a motion detector. The real problem would be when Dan opened the door. If it did have an alarm, that could trigger it and the four of us would have to fly across the field to get away. I wished that I had thought of that earlier. I should have told Dan to check for an alarm pad before opening an exterior door.

By the time we made it around back, Dan had the door open and I did not hear an alarm. Of course, it could be a silent one.

"I am going to make sure there isn't an alarm pad by the garage door," I said as they each stopped in their tracks.

I did not find any signs of an alarm and was shocked by my discovery. I know that there had to be thousands of dollars worth of furnishings sitting there unprotected. But I was also relieved.

The four of us started running in all directions, gathering piece after piece and bringing everything to the front door. The drive circled in front, making that the easiest exit. The garage was actually down several steps and the door position was awkward for moving the larger pieces. We would just have to risk going out the front.

For the next several minutes I would hear "Mine," "Dibs," "I want this," until I finally had enough.

"Just gather and load," I said. "We will choose later but for now we need to be quick."

Finally we had so much piled in the entrance hall and the adjoining living and dining rooms that I felt it was time to retrieve the vehicles.

"Why don't you two go? Leon and I will stay here and keep moving things near the front," said Dan.

I was not sure how I felt about leaving them. If the police came to check and the boys ran out the back, there would not be a car waiting for them. I looked at Bill, concerned.

"They will be okay," he said.

"Fine, we will be back as soon as we can. If you suspect any trouble at all, turn out the lights," I instructed. "If we see the house is totally dark, then we will go back to the road where we parked and pick you up. Okay?"

Bill and I hurried across the field. I would have sworn the acreage had expanded since we crossed it about 45 minutes earlier. It seemed to take forever to get to my car, but once we did, I drove Bill to his van.

"Remember, if the house is dark, turn around and go. I will hurry back to the road and pick them up, but you just go and get the hell away from here," I said. Talking about it made us both more nervous than we already were, but it was important that we had a plan.

I could see that the couple of lights were still on inside the house as I approached the cul-de-sac. Hopefully that meant they were safe. Once I was on the street, I turned my lights off and guided my car in by moonlight. Bill followed suit. We both pulled in the drive just as Leon opened the front door. You have never seen four sissies move as quickly as we did. The van was easy to load and I was grateful that I had recently traded my coupe in for a 1977 Pontiac Grand Safari station wagon. I had needed it in my design work and now, for the night shift.

Chairs, chests, lamps, pillows, drapes, bedspreads, a headboard, assorted tables, art, mirrors and even a loveseat made the first round. In spite of both vehicles being full, it still looked like we had barely made a dent in the available options inside. Dan jumped into the van with Bill and Leon got in the front seat of the station wagon with me. Since we did not have to break down the front door, we were able to close it. From the outside there was not a hint as to what had just transpired.

With our lights still off, I led the procession out of there. Once I turned onto the second street, I turned my headlights on and carefully drove away not wanting to attract any attention. Bill and I had both caked on mud to obscure some of the numbers on our license plates. If someone had noticed us, they would not have a full tag number to report.

Leon and I had cleaned out the garage in advance so that we could move and stack everything until we had a plan in place. We unloaded the big pieces in there and brought the smaller items and accessories inside. Our home looked like a furniture warehouse with beautiful accessories piled on every surface. It was after midnight and everything from the initial load was safe inside.

"Are we going back?" I asked although I already knew the answer.

All three said, "Yes," in unison.

"Okay, before we go, do we have a plan? Do you know what is left that you absolutely have to have or are we just going back for more, regardless?" I asked them.

"I wouldn't mind a side table that was upstairs in the front bedroom," said Leon.

"I would like that wicker rocking chair in the kid's room for my mom," Dan followed.

"I grabbed everything I really wanted with the first load," said Bill. "Anything now would just be icing on the cake. What about you?"

"Honestly, I don't know. I never got to see everything and can't think of anything that I have to have," I answered.

"Are you saying that you don't want to go back?" Leon asked me.

"No, just that I want to be very careful and not get greedy. You realize that there were times that the four of us were running around inside in every direction and that the police could have easily snuck up on us?" I said, letting it sink in for a minute. "We have to be more careful."

"Oh my God, you are right. No one was even watching. We were all so busy loading," Leon said as he grabbed my hand. "What do you suggest?"

"I think one of us, and it can be me, needs to stay outside in front by the cars. I can watch as well as help load if you guys bring it out. But not even for one second, should we all be inside and with no one on the lookout," I offered.

"I agree and I can do it," said Bill.

"No, I am fine being on watch but just wanted to put that out there," I countered.

"So, are we ready? And are we just going straight back there and hope for the best?" asked Dan.

"Yes, I think so, but we need to be as fast as we can. Even if we do not completely fill the vehicles, we cannot linger at all," I implored.

It was nearly one in the morning by the time we returned to the tour site. I noticed that the homes near the entrance of the subdivision had turned their interiors lights out, although a few had their exterior floodlights on. The collection of tour homes looked just the same, but it did not keep me from thinking cops could be hiding inside with their cars in the garage. I swear my mind could always go to the dark places. Or maybe I just kept thinking what I would do to catch criminals.

Again we pulled our vehicles in front and opened up the doors ready to load. I stayed outside keeping an eye on the street. I could see the road that led to the cul-de-sac. I was prepared to shut this down and get the hell out if I saw any headlights. The boys kept loading and I helped to position things in my car for the maximum advantage. And then I saw headlights in the distance.

"Car," I yelled and all three stopped what they were doing.

"Get ready to go," I instructed. But the car turned into the driveway of a house on the adjoining street. The lights disappeared around to the back and most likely into a garage. All three looked at me waiting for the go-ahead. Both vehicles were close to being full.

"Grab one more thing and then that is all," I said. "We have to go. It is really too dangerous."

No one argued with me. Bill went back for a small pull-up chair and Dan carried out a lamp. Seriously, just how many lamps were in that house? I kept waiting for Leon, who finally walked out with a fancy coffee maker that had been sitting on the kitchen counter. He shrugged his shoulders and smiled. I smiled back.

"Close and lock the door," I said adding, "Let's go."

Once again, with headlights off, we drove toward the entrance. Then with lights back on, we pulled onto the main street and headed home. There were very few cars on the road that time of morning. We made it safely back to my place shortly after two AM.

"I don't know where the rest of this stuff is going," I said as we got out of our vehicles.

"Let's unload your car and we can keep my van packed. I don't have a catering job tomorrow, or actually today, so we can put everything in our apartment," Bill said. "Later tonight, we can either start at your place or ours and begin dividing everything."

That sounded like a good plan to me. But the bigger question was where was everything going once things had been divided? By the time we got together later that night, Leon and I had decided a mini-warehouse was in our immediate future. Bill and Dan had come up with the same idea.

We picked up pizza for all of us on the way. They had the table set and drinks poured when we arrived. However, we all were so anxious that we fixed our plates and walked around looking at the pieces, which they had moved inside from their van.

"Does anyone else think that we're excessive? I mean, we don't even have places for all of this and now we are talking about renting mini-warehouses just to store everything," I said.

"I agree," said Dan. "It is crazy and maybe we should consider this our last run. Just how many end tables and lamps do we need? Plus, it is too dangerous to sell off anything that we just stole. I mean, that was such a huge hit that it is bound to attract some unwanted attention."

"Yeah, two cars plus two trips equals four loads," added Bill. "We seem to be escalating and I am afraid that we are getting careless. I did not even think about a lookout until Ricky mentioned it. That was just dumb. I don't want to go to jail."

"No one is going to jail. We got away with it. But I agree we should have been more careful," added Leon.

"I hate to ask this," Bill said, turning to Leon. "But did you touch any of the doorknobs or anything that we ended up leaving?"

"Why, Bill?" asked Leon.

"Because you were in jail and that means they have your fingerprints. Granted, with law enforcement in another state, but maybe you should have worn gloves. Hell, maybe we all should have worn gloves," Bill said getting flustered. "I mean, speaking of careless."

No one spoke as the magnitude of what Bill had just said began to sink in. He was right.

"We have been so cocky thinking that they wouldn't catch us. That we are indestructible, but we're not," I lamented.

"Don't panic, Ricky. First of all, there isn't anything we can do about it now – except be smarter moving forward," said Bill.

"I am not sure that we should move forward. We all just agreed that we have too much shit anyway," added Dan.

Snapping out of my panic, I realized that I needed to rein everyone in. I needed to be the voice of reason.

"Yes, we have made mistakes and yes, we have been lucky. Hopefully, our past actions won't bite us in the ass," I said and then continued. "I think that we need to divide everything and then put it in a warehouse. None of us needs any of this in our homes right now. Give it time to cool down and then swap things around. Let's wait two to three months before pulling it out. You know like the bank robbers always say on TV – they don't want to call attention to themselves by spending the loot immediately. I think that should be the same for us with this latest run. Let's let it simmer for a bit. I am going to go tomorrow and rent a place and then move whatever we end up with there for a while. What about you?"

"I think Ricky's right," said Bill looking at Dan. "Maybe we put it away until we buy a house and actually need it. Monthly warehouse rent is cheap compared to the legal fees we would have if we were arrested."

"Works for me," agreed Dan.

The three of us looked at Leon, who was still thinking about his fingerprints.

"Leon?" I asked.

"Yes, whatever you think is best. I am so sorry that I did not wear gloves. I would never want to bring trouble your way," Leon said remorsefully.

We made plans to rent warehouses immediately and not at the same business. Leon and I rented one near our condo and Bill knew of one near where his father lived across town.

It was time to divide everything but there was none of the excitement like in the past. It almost felt like drudgery, which was such a shame since everything was so beautiful. We took turns choosing. Leon and I had already made a few decisions earlier so that we could work in unison. I am pretty sure that Bill and Dan had as well.

There were things that I would have liked, but when you have so much, it does not seem worth fighting for. We kept it all very civil and fair. I thought later that there was another good reason for storing things for a while. With Greg coming back to town, I did not feel like showing off everything. I had already added quite a lot from the midnight runs with Bill and

Dan. I did not want him to be jealous of our added furnishings. After all, he had been out of the loop for about a year.

—•—

Greg came straight to our condo when he arrived in town with the plan to stay a night or two. He had worked it out with his brother, who would drive a rented truck with his furniture later, after he had rented an apartment. I had already scouted out a few possibilities, sent him information in advance, and lined up appointments to look at his favorites the following day.

At first I felt Leon and Greg were like a couple dogs ready to mark their territory, but it did not take long for Leon to charm him and for Greg to feel comfortable. Plus, they enjoyed ganging up on me in sharing embarrassing stories. I allowed them to amuse themselves for a while.

"Okay, that's enough. I have got my own stories to tell on each of you," I threatened.

I wondered how long it might take Greg to bring up the midnight runs. He had asked me a few weeks ago when we talked by phone if Leon knew about us. I had told him yes, but not everything.

He asked if Leon had been on a run with me. "Yes." Then he wanted to know if we had gone with Bill and Dan? "Yes." I could tell that upset him.

"Makes sense, seeing how you have totally redone everything while I was away," Greg said while checking out my condo. He did not act as if he thought that we should not have continued. More like he was sad that he had missed out — or maybe he felt Leon had taken his place.

Greg then asked me if I would help him get some things once he moved in. I said that I would do what I could, but more and more alarm systems were showing up in houses and fewer and fewer condos were setting up furnished models.

"I think the furniture stores are leery of putting their stuff in models because of damage and theft. I mean, how could we blame them?" I said. "The one thing that remains consistent are condominium clubhouses. They have to furnish them and if we get there early enough, before everything gets shopworn from use, then that might be a possibility." That seemed to appease him for now. But I knew that we would be talking about this again in the near future.

The next day Greg and I went to check out apartments. Leon had to go to work, but we said we would get together for dinner that night with Bill and Dan. Greg had several good apartment options and simply needed to narrow it down. The one that he ultimately chose would not have been my first choice. But then again, I was not going to live there. He signed a year's lease and it was available immediately.

That night he called his brother, who said he could drive his furniture up on the weekend. I told Greg that he was more than welcome to stay with us. Greg said that even though he started his new job on Monday, he would be fine at his new place once the furniture arrived.

Dan, Bill, Leon and I took Greg out to dinner that evening to his favorite "Fern Bar" where he had a frozen strawberry daiquiri along with dinner. We all joined him for cocktails and then Leon had another and then one more. His words were beginning to slur and I knew I needed to cut him off. It was getting harder and harder to do that. He was beginning to be resentful at being treated like a child. I did not want to be the parent but I also did not want him drunk.

I knew that he had a problem when we first met at the beach motel. I am not sure why I thought that he could change. For a while he controlled it, but recently he had been getting tipsy almost every night.

His drinking got worse after Bill had pointed out the carelessness of not wearing gloves. Leon took it personally because he not only put himself at risk but, felt he also put the rest of us in danger. I tried to comfort him and assure him that we would be okay, but the alcohol had a different plan. At first, he would be apologetic and mad at himself but as he continued to drink, the tables would turn and Leon would blame me for putting him in that position.

I knew that he did not mean it and when he was sober he would say that he was sorry. And yet, it was beginning to happen more and more, like a recurring nightmare, and I did not know how to fix it.

There had been times where Greg or I had been plastered, either separately or together, but not on a nightly basis. My concerns with a drunk Leon was one, he ran his mouth too much and I never knew what might spill out; and two, he did not need to be hung over working at the religious publishing house.

"This was great but maybe we should call it an early night," I said and Greg agreed, as did Bill and Dan. I guided Leon to the car and we came home.

Greg's brother arrived on Saturday afternoon and all of us helped unload the truck into Greg's new apartment. We did not bother to place everything because his brother was tired and it was getting late. I promised to come by the next morning and help arrange and decorate. By the time I arrived the next day, his brother had already left. That was fine since I really did not get along with him all that well. Like Greg's mother, he thought that I was a bad influence on Greg too. He just did not know how bad!

I let Leon sleep in, but I left a note telling him where I was and that I hoped that he would come over later. He showed up around lunchtime and offered to go pick up Thai takeout and we all agreed that it sounded good. It was the early 1980s and our city had only one decent Thai restaurant. But their Green Curry was excellent.

Greg did not have a phone yet and the phone company said it would be Wednesday midday before they could put one in. Since Greg would be at work, I offered to meet the installer if the apartment manager was unable to let them in. He had already put the utilities in his name and mail had been forwarded. With the furniture in place and the pictures hung, it was clear that he had room for a few more things.

He had rented a two-bedroom unit but was not planning on having a roommate. I knew that it wouldn't be long before the midnight run conversation would come up again and I was dreading it. I did not want to go back out there. The four of us were still sitting on our last haul and paying a monthly fee to keep it hidden in storage. I also did not know if I could help Greg without involving everyone else. With five of us, it would become a huge production.

Chapter Fifteen

Although it might have been difficult for others to fully understand how we could afford the extravagance displayed in our homes in the 1980s, at least by then, we each had decent jobs, steady incomes and a more comfortable lifestyle – with the exception of Dean.

"Dean's back," said Greg stopping by my studio.

"What do you mean, he's back? He's married. I was at his wedding wearing that ugly tux and trying not to fall out laughing when his two fat sisters sang that awful duet," I explained.

"I know. I was there, too. But he is getting a divorce," Greg continued. "He got caught messing around."

"With a man?" I asked.

"No, a woman," Greg replied.

"So that man thing was just a phase during college?" I said.

"I guess so," he answered.

"Greg, did he ask to move in with you?" I asked.

"Yes."

"And you are going to do it, aren't you?" I continued.

"Yes."

"You know that he is probably going to leave you in a bind again?" I said.

Greg went on to explain that it would different this time. Dean would be moving into his place and not talking Greg into something that he would be unable afford on his own. Greg was now financially able to live by himself so if Dean moved out in a month or so, Greg would still be fine. Plus, I think that he just wanted the company.

"Okay, just be careful. And don't let him take advantage of you," I said with concern.

—•—

I was grateful that Greg had not brought up going on a midnight run again. However, I could still feel his request hanging over my head. Bill, Dan, Leon and I had things from the last haul still in storage and yet I sensed Bill was itching to pull a few of their pieces out of hiding. It had been almost three months and even I was feeling more comfortable with the thought that we had gotten away with it. I asked Bill and Dan to hold off for a little while longer until I could find something quick and easy to appease Greg. Reluctantly, they said yes.

"I think that we should go with you if you are doing another run," Bill said with a gleam in his eye.

"Why? You don't need a thing? It would be an unnecessary risk for you and for us," I said.

"Or, it would mean more for you and Greg if you did not have to split it with us," said Bill.

"I don't need anything. You don't need anything. We all have more than we can even use. Hell, we are even paying storage fees just because we have no place to put everything," I continued.

"We are looking at houses and think that we have found one. It is in rough shape but huge. A real fixer-upper," Dan said excitedly.

"Well, that's news to me," I said looking at Bill.

"So you see, we will soon have room for everything and a little bit more," Bill added.

"Okay guys, I have not found anything yet that I feel good about. No one is building now," I explained.

The four of us were in my home sitting in my living room, where I would sometimes catch myself staring in disbelief at the sheer gorgeousness of it all. The rust velvet sofa sitting on the antique Persian rug in navy and burnt orange. The antique lowboy with the burl-wood top. The gilt mirror hanging above reflecting the crystal lamp, brass candlesticks and leather-bound books. Original art and beautifully framed signed etchings hung on cobalt lacquered walls. It was a magazine-worthy room that would never be photographed. And yet, I was able to enjoy it daily.

Leon turned toward me and joined in the conversation.

"But you told Greg clubhouses might be an option," he said.

"And they are, but did you see anything worth taking in the few that we checked out?" I asked.

"No," Leon said now looking over at Bill and Dan. "They really are putting crappy furniture in some of the clubhouses. I guess they know that it is going to get wear and tear so no need to do anything nice. Plus, everything is now mauve. Mauve and gray. Mauve and teal. I mean, call it what it really is – pink on pink with an accent of pink."

"I think I know of a place," said Bill, still laughing at Leon's comment. "I have not said anything because it is a little bit out of our usual comfort zone."

"How much out?" I asked.

"It's an interior design studio," Bill said.

"No, absolutely not. I am an interior designer. I probably know this person. No way," I said raising my voice. "Who is it?"

Bill mentioned the name and immediately I had mixed feelings. I did not know him personally, but certainly knew all about him. He was the joker who stole pieces from Palmer's and then went out on his own and was stupid enough to let the newspaper photograph his home with the hot merchandise in plain view.

"Well, that certainly makes it a little more interesting," I admitted. "But really guys, if word got out that I had anything to do with it, I would be finished in the design business."

"Girl, you would be finished, period! We all would, if we got caught," Dan added to the conversation.

"Okay," I relented. "I am not saying yes, until I know more."

Bill went on to tell us what he knew. One of the jobs that he catered recently was at a home that was redecorated by the designer in question. Bill had complimented his client, which led her to go on and on about how wonderful her interior designer was. She added that he was opening his own studio nearby.

Curious, Bill and Dan rode by the new location one night. It was located on what had been a residential street that had recently turned commercial. Some of the small houses had been torn down for new buildings, while others had been remodeled for commercial use, which was the case of his design studio. It was originally a small duplex with a new display window added in front. There were four exterior doors since both units had a front and back door. Looking through the windows, Bill could see that the pair of units had been combined into one larger space. He also saw several tasty little items that he wanted.

"You were planning on doing this without us, weren't you?" I asked Bill.

"Is that true?" Leon chimed in.

"No," said Dan, coming to Bill's rescue. "We just found out about it the other day and had not had the chance to tell you. We were still scouting it out to learn everything before presenting the idea."

Later, when Leon and I were alone, we agreed that we did not believe Bill and Dan for a minute. But if the situation were reversed, would we have told them about it?

"The problem is," Bill, continued. "It's a small space with barely enough inventory to make the four of us happy, much less Greg. I will go ahead and say that there is a stunning desk in the front window, which I am calling dibs on right here and now."

"Okay, Leon and I will go by and take a look and get back with you. It sounds promising, but it doesn't help my situation with Greg," I said.

"I'll tell you what, you help us on this job and we will help you on the next one and make sure that Greg is taken care of," said Bill. "Will that work?"

As it turned out, neither Bill nor Dan appeared to trust us to go look on our own. They wanted to ride along. I couldn't believe that they were afraid that we might hit the studio without them. I parked my car a couple of doors down in a parking lot by one of the new buildings. There were several cars already in the lot and we blended right in.

Then the four of us walked over to the design studio, which was lit from inside with expensive looking lamps. Fortunately, there was not a single car or exterior light in sight. I am sure that the designer felt by leaving lamps on that it would entice people to look in the windows and see what he had to offer. It definitely had that effect on us – but not for the purpose intended. The desk Bill wanted, positioned in the front window, was unique and lovely. I can see why he was attracted to it. But I was also able to see from where I stood a console, chest, several lamps and original artwork.

Walking around the building to peer into windows, I saw the kitchen and a bath. I could also see an office in what had probably been a former bedroom. There were two other windows that were dark and there was no way of telling what treasures those rooms held. I did not see an alarm sticker and the original exterior doors looked easy enough to bump. Other than the new display window in front, the remaining windows looked original to the house and were painted shut. I said that I preferred going through the kitchen door in the back because we could already see into that room with no surprises. The other two doors could have been blocked from inside or nailed shut as far as we knew, since there was no way for us to see which rooms they opened into.

Once we were back in my car, I shared my ideas and asked if everyone agreed.

"When do you think would be a good time to hit it?" asked Bill.

"Why not tonight?" I replied.

"And what about Greg?" Bill asked.

"You were right, there is barely enough for all of us, unless those two dark rooms hold more inventory," I answered.

"Are you okay with not including Greg?" Dan asked, turning to me.

"Yes, this was your find, not mine. I appreciate that you are letting Leon and I join in the fun. If there had been more, I would have wanted to include Greg. But as things are, I think it should be just the four of us," I said. "Let's just promise not to brag about in front of Greg. Agreed?"

Everyone was on board with the plan as we went back to retrieve the catering van. Since we were not sure what might be in the other two rooms, Leon and I took my Grand Safari just in case. Once again, we parked two doors down until we had everything ready to load.

The old kitchen door gave way with just a couple of bumps and little noise. I quickly looked for an alarm keypad by the door but did not find one. Bill and Dan rushed into the front room and turned off the lamps. With that new display window, anyone driving by would have been able to see us moving things around. Fortunately, the streetlights offered just enough of a glow to work by. Bill and Dan moved the desk near the back door as Leon and I grabbed the console. Then the chest, chairs, art and remaining lamps. We had the front room emptied and everything positioned in the back. The kitchen offered nothing nor did the bath. One of the dark rooms turned out to be wall-to-wall shelves of fabric and wallpaper sample books. And then I opened the door to the last room and my heart stopped. There was a twin bed, TV, nightstand with an alarm clock and clothes in the closet.

"He lives here," I called out.

"What?" asked Bill from the hallway.

"I said he lives here. This is his bedroom, his clothes," I added.

Bill was standing by the bathroom door. He walked in and opened the linen closet.

"There are toiletries in here. Oh shit," Bill said starting to panic.

"What do we do?" yelled Dan.

"We get the hell out of here," I said. "Now."

All four of us stumbled over the pile of furniture as we fought to reach the back door. I was the last one out, closed the door and followed the others toward our vehicles. We all took a deep breath and waited for our pulsing heartbeats to slow down.

"Don't we need to go?" asked Leon.

"Yes, but let me suggest something. We could hit it fast and hard," I said.

All three looked at me as if I had lost my mind. And then Dan started to open his mouth and I put my hand up.

"It is a huge risk," I continued. "Dangerous. We do not know if he might come back in ten minutes or tomorrow. Hell, he could be out of town. He may even live somewhere else but has this for a getaway. There are so many unknowns. Still, there is not that much there and it will all fit in the van. I say we go in and grab the desk, the chest, the console, that small chair and then everyone gets either a lamp or painting and then we run as fast as we can. Five minutes tops."

Still in shock by our discovery, it took a moment for my plan to sink in. But then everyone thought about it and they realized that it might work.

"I'm game," said Leon.

"Well, we're here, queer, willing and able," muttered Dan before turning to Bill.

"Why not?" said Bill after an exaggerated pause.

For just a split-second, I thought to myself: *What have I just done?*

Bill got into his van and moved it near the back door. The three us walked over quickly to join him. With the vehicle doors swung open wide, Bill and Dan loaded in the desk while Leon and I brought out the console. Next the chest went in and then the chair. Leon and I had a lamp in each hand and Dan was holding a large oil landscape. Bill snatched up a pair of oversized candlesticks and had a shopping bag with who knows what.

Leon and I followed Bill and Dan back to their apartment and parked our vehicles.

"Why don't we make our choices now and not carry everything upstairs? There really aren't that many items," I suggested.

"Perfect," said Dan.

"Bill, you should go first," I suggested.

"Thanks. The desk. Ricky?" asked Bill.

"The console," I said. I really wanted the chest, too. Leon and I had discussed it on the way over but the next turn went to Dan.

"I'd like the landscape," said Dan.

"The chest," said Leon, giving me a wink. We were both pleasantly surprised with Dan's choice.

Anything after that did not really matter to me. We ended up with a pair of lamps and an inlaid box that Bill had tossed into the shopping bag on his last trip.

We transferred the console and the rest of the items into my car, with the exception of the chest. Bill said that he could run it over tomorrow after lunch. I thanked him and thought to myself, we now have even more stuff that we don't need. And I still have not helped Greg find anything for his place.

Chapter Sixteen

Dean ended up moving in with Greg. He had walked out of his marriage with just the clothes on his back and a TV, which he had put in Greg's spare bedroom. I hoped that things would work out with the two of them living together but I had reservations from our past experiences.

Somewhere along the way, Dean had put two and two together and asked for confirmation about our nighttime activities. He did not know and probably would never comprehend the full extent of our thefts. But he was intrigued and appeared willing to learn. If we added Dean to the mix, the midnight run equation would max out at six.

I felt sure that he would want to go with Greg and me on the next run, however, I still had not found anything that was tempting enough for us to even make an effort.

Leon and I invited Dean and Greg over for dinner one night. Dean had found a job at a music store for minimum wage. He had previously been working for his father-in-law's company and had made good money. Now he was back scraping by like a college student. I knew that he was miserable and prayed that he would land on his feet soon.

After dinner, Leon and Dean decided to play a game that involved each of them drinking shots. I think that they would purposely lose just so they could down another. In no time at all, they were both drunk, loud and obnoxious.

"It's Leon's fault," said Greg.

I did not disagree but still Greg's comment made me angry.

"Dean did not need much encouragement," I countered.

"He is unhappy, divorced and in a dead end job. It doesn't take much to put him over the edge," Greg said, thinking that justified Dean's behavior.

"We need to put a stop to this," I said. "I'll get Leon. You take Dean."

Neither one was happy about the interference. Leon was already headed toward one of his meltdowns that happened whenever his booze was cut off – the fighting, the name-calling. I knew what drama to expect and did not look forward to it.

Greg and Dean had come in Dean's car, but wisely, Greg took the keys as we both coaxed Dean into the passenger seat. I am sure Greg had his hands full when they got home. But then, so did I. Once they had left, Leon stretched out on the sofa and promptly passed out leaving me with the chore of cleaning up everything from dinner. Normally I would have gathered Leon up, undressed him and helped him into bed. But tonight, it just was not worth it. I deserved a good night's rest and if that meant sleeping in separate rooms, then so be it.

I didn't care anymore. Immediately, I felt a shudder run down my spine when I had that thought. *I just did not care anymore.*

—●—

Greg started pressing me to help him find a few things. He wanted outdoor furniture for his balcony and a table and chairs for his dining room.

"Been down that road before with Jim and Jack," I stated. "I wonder what ever became of those tired old queens. Seems like a lifetime ago."

"Do you ever think that our luck is about to run out?" Greg asked.

"All the time," I replied.

I told Greg that outdoor furniture was easy. Every condo and apartment complex with a swimming pool had something. And now that it was fall, most likely no one would be using it. I thought that I knew of the perfect spot in a small complex close to town. They did have a pool, but there was also a private terrace area with a gas grill between two of the condo buildings. And unlike pool areas, there was not the obstacle of a fence to deal with.

"How do you know about it?" Greg was curious.

"I had a client who lived there at one time but they have since moved. We will have to carry the stuff quite a distance back to the parking lot. But I remember it being a fairly quiet complex with older residents," I answered.

"I hope they are not snoopy old busybodies like us," Greg chuckled. "Sounds like it is worth checking out."

"What about Dean?" I asked. "Should we include him?"

"He is going to find out as soon as we bring anything home," Greg said matter-of-factly. "What do you think?"

"I think there will be a table and four chairs that could get loaded faster with three people instead of two. So, yes, I think that you should ask him," I answered, hoping that Greg would agree.

"Okay, but first, let's make sure that it is all still there and that we feel comfortable with it," he said.

It was late afternoon and the sun was going down by the time we rode over and found a parking spot. Neither one of us thought we would draw much attention to ourselves if we did a quick walk through. As it turned out, there was indeed a wrought iron table and four chairs in good condition, just as I had remembered, on a small slab of concrete with a gas grill nearby. It was a longer walk than I preferred back to where we could park our car. But still, it was doable.

"Will Leon join us?" Greg asked.

"I would rather not ask him," I said.

"Are you two okay?"

"Sure." I tried to say convincingly. "But this is for you and he might think something should be in it for him. Let me help you and Dean and we do not have to mention anything to Leon."

"Okay, thanks," said Greg.

My only problem with that plan was that Leon was usually home at night getting drunk. He would question where I was going that late but on the other hand, he might be passed out and never know anything about it. Normally I would try to keep him from drinking himself to the point of being unconscious but tonight, I would let him do his thing, pass out and I hoped that he would never know anything about it.

True to what had now become his norm, Leon started drinking as soon he got home from work. He went through the stages of being charming, then affectionate, then sloppy, followed by belligerent before passing out. He had now moved into the hostile stage in the anticipation of me cutting him off, but I did not do it this time. I thought to myself, drink up. It was now nine-thirty and soon he was already snoring on the sofa.

"I'm ready and will come pick you up," I said as soon as Greg answered the phone.

Dean and Greg came bounding down to the car dressed in dark, yet, still fashionable, attire – our standard "work" uniform. We arrived at our destination shortly after ten. Dean was worried that might be too early, thinking some of the homeowners would still be up. However, being a place geared more for seniors, there were only a couple of units that still had lights on and those residents were probably watching the evening news before turning in.

I pulled into the closest parking space I could find and took the light bulb out of the overhead interior ceiling light. I had learned that trick a while back so that when we opened the car doors, nothing illuminated the interior. I can't believe it took me so long to catch on.

The three of us slipped behind the buildings headed for the patio area. I thought we needed to load the table first followed by the chairs. Greg and Dean each grabbed the table but Dean stumbled and dropped it on its side. A light went on in the closest condo and I heard a door open.

"What's going on?" a man's voice yelled in the dark.

Damn. This never happens.

"Run," I implored. We hightailed it out of there as fast as we could, jumped in my car and I tore out of the parking lot.

"Well, that did not go as planned," I said. We all started laughing nervously.

"Way to go, klutz," Greg said turning to look at Dean.

Dean started apologizing.

"It's okay, we got away. It could have happened to any of us," I said, meaning every word.

Still Dean was upset that he had blown the chance of picking up the outdoor table and chairs. I assured him there would be other opportunities.

When I got home I saw that Leon was just as I had left him – sprawled across the sofa snoring. I looked at him and at my velvet sofa and thought, there will come a day that I am going to have to reupholster it. But not until that boy can sober up for good.

I had made the mistake one day of suggesting to Leon that he might consider rehab. I was sincere and willing to help with the expense if he would agree. It ended up being our biggest fight ever and almost turned violent. I had embarrassed Leon by saying this in front of Bill and Dan but at the time, I felt I needed their support. When Dan realized how badly it was going he stepped in and took Leon's side – not because he thought that I was wrong, but because he saw the fear in Leon's eyes and knew that he needed a friend. I never brought the subject up again.

I was determined to find patio furniture for Greg and Dean and spent most of my free time over the next few days riding around checking out anything and everything. But before I found a replacement, I found a pair of statues that I loved. I should say "we" found them, as in Leon and myself. We had been out to lunch on a Saturday and he wanted to go riding around. I was enjoying driving in and out of neighborhoods when I spotted something new.

The latest home craze in town was the "cluster." Oversized homes were being built on teeny-tiny lots. Unlike condominiums, the homeowner would be responsible for the outside upkeep of their home. One of my favorite old mansions in town now had excavation going on with roads being built on the surrounding vast acreage. It appeared that they were not planning to tear down the original estate but simply surround it with new cluster homes, leaving practically no remaining green space.

A couple of houses were already in the early stages of construction but I drove past them and stopped in front of the existing mansion. I had admired it from afar for so many years and now saw that it was clearly vacant. I felt a surge of excitement as we got out of the car. Peering through the windows and French doors, we saw how grand everything was. Marble mantels, herringbone oak floors, elegant doorknobs, chandeliers and sconces. We tried every possible way in but all the doors and windows were locked. Leon really wanted inside and was ready to break in any way that he could.

"No," I said. I could not bear the thought of damaging this Grand Dame. "We can keep checking back and I bet we will eventually catch it unlocked or a key hidden."

That did not appease Leon but at the moment he was sober, so his common sense kicked in and he decided it was better not to argue. I wondered if he would come back on his own. *Had it really reached the point that I did not trust Leon anymore?*

"Let's check it out," I said, pointing toward the garden with a wrought iron gazebo as a centerpiece.

I could tell that he was not ready to give up on the idea of breaking into the mansion, but he reluctantly followed me. What we had been unable to see till now was a pair of statues. They appeared to be Roman figures painted black.

"I want them," said Leon, more animated than I had seen him in some time.

"Okay, but can you lift it?" I asked agreeing that they were wonderful. He tried and would have succeeded but most likely would have also strained something.

"Stop, let me help," I offered. Together we carried one statue to my car and then the other. I hated to take them away from their garden setting. But I told myself that there would be a good chance that if we didn't, someone else would. So I was able to justify the theft by thinking of it as historical preservation.

We placed the stately pair of statues on each side of our fireplace. It was an amazing find and totally unexpected. I knew Bill would have a few catty remarks to make once he saw them, all the while trying to hide his jealousy. Again, as thrilled as I was, it just reminded me of Greg and the obligation that I felt to help him. I did not intentionally plan to keep adding to our stash, but things just worked out that way.

—●—

Leon got a call that evening from a friend of his back home and they talked for nearly an hour. I was curious but he remained somewhat tight-lipped about the gist of their conversation, other than to say that I had met his friend on that momentous trip to the beach. I knew that Leon, like me, had been there with friends but I had never spent any time with them. I only remembered seeing a couple of guys on that first day by the pool. I had not thought much about it, but now I realized that Leon rarely talked about his friends or his life back home.

"You said that was Freddy?" I asked.

"Yeah."

"Was he the tall one with brown hair or the shorter blonde dude?" I continued, trying to place his friend from that trip.

"Tall."

"Well, aren't you a wealth of information?" I said sarcastically.

Leon finally added that his friends were planning a party in a few weeks and that they wanted him to come to town for it. They were expecting a bunch of other friends to be there, several of which Leon had not seen in a long time.

"Do you want to go?" I asked.

"Yes," Leon said defiantly.

"Did they invite me?"

Silence.

"Oh."

"You can come if you want to but you won't know anyone," he offered reluctantly.

I had mixed feelings. I did not really want to go. But I also was not happy with being excluded by the man I was supposed to be in a relationship with. I decided that I really needed to make the effort and meet his friends.

"I would like to go, if that would be okay with you," I stated.

"Sure. Whatever," he replied without an ounce of sincerity.

Wow! That really made me feel wanted. I admitted to myself that I had turned into a nag over his drinking and that it had put a strain on our relationship. I promised myself that if I went, Leon could do whatever he wanted. I would make sure that he enjoyed himself. I did not want to be seen as the harpy housewife.

The next two weeks were routine. As predicted, Bill and Dan had much to say about our latest additions. Dan went on and on about how much he loved them and true to form, Bill made several snide remarks, which in "Bill speak" meant he was so jealous that he could not bring himself to even fake saying something nice. I took it as a huge compliment.

Leon continued to drink each evening but not to the point of passing out. However, he did go out one evening to our local gay bar without me and did not come home until after it had closed around three in the morning. I was worried to death about him driving drunk and I was fearful that he might hurt himself or someone else. It was a chore to get him out of bed three hours later and ready for work.

I could only imagine what a joy it must have been for his co-workers to be around him that day. As for me, I was just grateful to have him out of the house.

—●—

I found another patio furniture option for Greg and Dean and they were raring to go. I decided that I needed to ask Leon to join us, but secretly hoped that he would say no.

"Why are you helping them? What's in it for you?" asked Leon sharply.

"One, they are my friends. And two, I offered to help Greg when he moved back to town. He still doesn't have a clue just how much we have in storage so I feel like it is the least that I can do," I explained.

"What difference does it make how much we have? He was not even around when we got most of it," Leon sputtered.

"I know. But again, he is my friend and I offered to help. You are welcome to join us or not. It is up to you. But there is not anything in it for us other than good will," I replied.

"No, go do your thing, but be careful. If you get arrested, it will come back to me and I don't want to go back to jail."

Was this the same guy I thought was so sweet and thoughtful at one time? Was I that bad a judge of character or had he changed that much? And if so, was I the reason why? Did I do something to cause him to act this way? Or am I just now seeing the real Leon?

Yes, I knew from the start, but I tried to ignore his drinking problem. Even when he was drunk, he had never been mean or spiteful until recently. Was he simply reacting to my actions? To my attempt at intervention? Or to my complaining? And if so, could I change my attitude – or had we gone too far down this road to turn around and make it right?

I found myself tormented with doubt and confusion. Was this my fault? Or was Leon damaged and I had failed to see until now?

—●—

The days had gotten much shorter and it was now dark by four in the afternoon. I told Greg and Dean that we could go as soon as they got home from work.

"Why so early? Is it safe?" asked Greg.

"I would not risk it if it weren't," I replied.

I felt comfortable with the job because it was a home and the people had apparently moved out. I assumed that the realtor had convinced them to leave a few things inside and outside so that the house would show better. I had looked through the windows earlier and saw that there was a pair of chairs, a lamp in the living room, and a large round table in the dining room draped in a silk plaid skirt. I could not tell if there was anything else that had been left since I had not been able to go inside. If a key had been hidden, then it was hidden really well.

I did not want to break in until we were ready to go. However, the main attraction and the immediate need was the wrought iron round table with four chairs on the patio. There were also a couple of matching chaise lounge chairs with a small concrete table positioned between them.

Because of the setting, I thought that we would be fine going by earlier rather than waiting until late into the night. Maybe I needed to change our name to *Nathaniel and the Late Afternoon Movers*, although it did not have the same ring to it.

We took my station wagon and I drove around to the back of the house. My plans were simple – grab the things off of the terrace and go. I did not feel like it was worth breaking into the house for what little I had seen through the windows. However, when Greg looked through the windows, he said that he loved the fabric-covered dining table and would like to have it. He thought that we could always come up with some chairs later.

"We can't get both tables and the patio chairs in the car at the same time. In fact, I am not sure that we can get the dining table in my car at all. It looks like it would be too wide," I said.

"It might come apart," suggested Greg.

"Maybe so, but we won't know until we break down a door," I countered.

"Okay, let's get the stuff off the patio and then think about the other," Dean said looking at Greg for confirmation.

We moved very quickly picking up and loading the wrought iron set into my car. I asked Greg if he also wanted the chaise lounge chairs, thinking that we would have to make another trip. I was relieved when he said that his balcony was not wide enough to use them.

The three of us had to ride in the front seat together because of everything we had in the back of my car. I was glad to have at least one of Greg's requests marked off of my to-do list.

"I really think that I would like that dining table," Greg said on the way home. "Can we go back after we unload?"

"Okay," I answered reluctantly.

After carrying the lawn furniture upstairs and placing it on Greg's balcony, we got back in my car and returned to the scene of the crime, but the police had beat us to it. I saw flashing blue lights ahead in the darkness and realized that they were in front of the home where we had just been. Clearly a neighbor must have spotted us and called it in because we had not broken down a door or set off an alarm.

I did not want to drive past the house so I pulled into a driveway a few doors down and hoped that no one would notice. The drive circled in front and came back out onto the street where I turned and headed away from the flashing lights.

"That was too close," said Greg.

"I just hope that whoever called it in did not get a look at my license tag," I added.

"Why did we do this?" asked Dean, still in shock. "I knew it was a bad idea. And I knew that we went too early. It was just dumb."

"Shut up. You are not helping matters," Greg said.

"First of all, if they saw my tag, they will come after me, not you," I added. "And I would take the blame."

"But we have the stolen goods, not you," said Dean.

I could not argue with them. My mind was so scrambled at the moment that I did not dare.

"It is going to be okay. You will see. Don't panic. And do not say anything to Leon or Bill and Dan," I said. "It would only get them worked up for no reason. We don't know if the cops even have a clue that it was us. And hell, it was just a table and chairs."

"I know," said Dean. "Just a table and chairs that we could have bought or done without. It was not worth the risk."

Neither Greg nor I had a good rebuttal. It was true. Every time that we did another job we put ourselves at risk. And for what? A crappy table and chairs not worth more than a couple of hundred dollars at the most.

Chapter Seventeen

Leon was still awake and halfway sober when I got home.

"How did it go?" he asked.

"Fine, they now have a wrought iron table and chairs for their balcony," I replied.

"Well, la-de-da. So, are you done now?" Leon asked in a snippy tone.

"Not quite, I told them that I would try to find a table and chairs for their dining room, too. Then, I think I will be done," I answered, trying to not let his tone bother me.

"If you find a furnished model that has more than just a table and chairs, then I will help," he offered.

"Because you want something too?" I asked. "Where would we put one more thing?"

"It doesn't matter. More is never enough," he answered.

I thought to myself, *what have I created?*

—●—

The following weekend we packed Leon's car and drove six hours for a party that I could have cared less about attending, but felt that I needed to go if only to keep an eye on Leon. I remembered the fun that we used to have in the car together. I tried to keep a conversation going but he would just give me one-word replies, which made it perfectly clear that he had no intention of being engaging. However, when we finally reached his friend Freddy's home, it was like someone had flipped on a switch. Leon became animated, charming and more like the guy I had met and fell in love with on that beach trip a few years earlier.

Freddy was polite and cordial to me but I still felt like an outsider. He had a very nice home, which I learned had been bought with a generous inheritance. It was furnished with a mixture of antiques that I assumed were family pieces and accented with contemporary art. I hated to admit it but I was impressed. It was done in excellent taste.

The house had four bedrooms and three baths. We were assigned one guest room and told that the other out-of-town friends would be staying in the remaining two bedrooms. The party was the following night and the additional houseguests would not arrive until tomorrow.

Lucky us, Leon and I had the house to ourselves. Or I should say, I had the place to myself. Leon and Freddy were so deep into conversation and inside jokes that they were oblivious to me. However, I reminded myself that I would not complain. I wanted Leon to have a wonderful time in hopes that he would come home in a much better mood than when he left.

The three of us went out to dinner and met up with another couple. One of the pair was Martin, who turned out to be the shorter, blond friend from the first beach vacation. His companion Marc, who made it clear to me that they were just friends, proceeded to rest his hand on my thigh under the table throughout most of our meal. While I appreciated the attention, I wondered if it had been planned. Maybe Leon wanted to have someone tempt me to see if I would follow through. I did not resist but I also did not give any encouragement.

Leon and Freddy had cocktails before we had left the house. Now they were sharing their second bottle of wine at the restaurant. Martin had joined them on the first bottle but declined any more. Martin's friend, Marc (which he made sure to tell me was spelled with a 'c') stopped after one glass, as did I.

"Not a big drinker?" Marc asked me.

"No, been tapering off these days," I said.

"Someone needs to stay sober, I guess," he continued, as he turned his head and nodded in the direction of Leon and Freddy.

"I guess," I added, curious as to where this conversation was headed.

"No fun being the adult," he said.

I was not sure just how drunk Freddy and Leon were, but I did not want to be overheard complaining about them. So I changed the subject.

"What do you do, Marc?" I asked.

"I am an interior designer. In fact, you have seen my work," he replied.

"Ah… Freddy's?" I asked.

"Yes."

"You are very talented. His home is striking. I am an interior designer, too," I admitted.

"I know. I saw pictures of your place that Leon mailed to Freddy a while back," said Marc.

What? I had no idea that Leon had photographed our place, much less shared the photos with anyone. Leon was aware of that designer who had gotten in trouble by letting the newspaper do a story with photos of his stolen furnishings. The same designer whose studio/ residence we had hit not that long ago.

In fact, all of my midnight crew had agreed to no photos, period.

Inwardly I was about to explode at Leon's carelessness, his stupidity. I was sure he thought he was rebelling against my steadfast rule and at the same time, against me. And yet, I doubt that he realized what the consequences of his actions might mean for all of us.

It took all of my acting skills just to keep my face from betraying the frustration that I felt.

"You didn't know?" he asked with concern.

"No, but I'm glad you like our place," I said, trying to recover from the shock.

"I love that burl-top lowboy and gilt mirror that you have. And Freddy could not get over those Roman statues by your fireplace. Very handsome," he said.

"Thank you."

"We will have to compare notes one day," he suggested. Which I took to mean we would be comparing other things as well, because his hand had just moved upward on my thigh.

Leon was in no condition to talk about anything by the time we got back to Freddy's home. I was still so mad from learning about the photographs that it was probably better that way. I held my tongue, helped put him to bed and went to sleep fuming.

Leon had his usual hangover the next morning but Freddy was alert, looked rested and had coffee made. He was also in the process of whipping up French toast for our breakfast when I walked into the kitchen.

"Sleep well?" Freddy asked.

"Yes, thank you. I really enjoyed the restaurant last night," I said. "Thank you for dinner."

"Sure, it also looked like you were enjoying Marc as well," Freddy said with a wink.

Crap, had I really been that obvious?

"Just showing a little southern hospitality," I said with a smile.

Leon stumbled into the room and we both looked in his direction. Freddy took the words right out of my mouth.

"You look like hell," he said.

"I usually don't drink that much," Leon said with a straight face.

Did he really say that? Who does he think he's kidding? There were so many bitchy comments going through my head that I was dying to say. *No, Ricky. Don't do it, Ricky. It is not worth it, Ricky.*

Again, Freddy conveyed my sentiments with one word.

"Bullshit," Freddy mumbled.

"How can I help with the party tonight?" I was hoping to change the subject.

"Thanks, but it's under control. The caterers will be here around three to set up and our other out-of-town guests hope to arrive by one. I thought that we might have a late lunch, if that is okay with the two of you," said Freddy.

"Sure," Leon sputtered.

"Sounds perfect, Freddy. Thanks so much for everything," I said. I hoped that my acting skills had not failed me and that my words rang with sincerity, in spite of how hollow they felt to me.

We had a rather lazy morning and did not get cleaned up until close to noon. The other two couples arrived together. There were two men and two women and I was not immediately sure if they were straight or gay couples. However, the women did show affection to each other and held hands when they went down the hall to their room, so I assumed that the men were a couple as well. It turned out that they were and both had gone to school with Freddy and Leon, although one of the two was a couple of classes behind them. Fortunately, they seemed nice and I did not feel as if they had any sort of agenda towards me.

Since they all knew each other and had known each other for years, they fell into comfortable conversations. I felt left out. But again, I smiled, joined in when I could and acted like a team player. It helped to realize that Leon probably felt the same way when he first entered my life with my friends.

Freddy had prepared in advance a shrimp salad with fresh fruit and Italian bread for our lunch, along with a very tasty cheesecake. His dining room table was large enough to seat all of us and I actually was beginning to relax and enjoy myself. The caterers arrived as we were clearing the table.

The two couples, tired from the drive that morning, wanted to rest up a bit before the evening's activity. Freddy felt like he needed be there to supervise the caterers. Leon asked if I would like for him to show me around.

"Yes, that would be wonderful," I said, hopeful for a pleasant afternoon.

We got into his car and Leon gave me a tour of the town. His school, the house where he had lived, a clothing store that had been his first job in high school. It was a lovely afternoon and although I knew better than to bring it up, I just could not help myself.

"Marc told me he saw photos of our home that you had sent to Freddy," I said.

"So?"

"I was just surprised because I thought that we had all decided that it would be risky having pictures of our things out there. You never know who might recognize something," I continued.

"I did not decide anything. You decided, like you always do." Leon snapped.

Uh oh, I knew that tone.

"And I did not show them to just anyone, I showed them to my friends," he added.

I wanted to say so much more but realized that I had already said too much. I let the subject drop. But Leon's mood had already changed. He drove us back to Freddy's home and my tour abruptly came to an end.

"Everything okay?" Freddy asked as we walked through the door. He could already sense Leon was upset about something.

"Thank you. Yes, looking forward to tonight," I was trying to keep up pretenses.

Leon felt the need to contradict me. "Ricky was pissed that I sent you photos of our home – or should I say, his home?" he said.

Wow, where did that come from?

"I am sorry but no, I was not upset," I responded. "I was just surprised when Marc told me about them. I did not know that you had done that. It's fine."

"I don't know everything that you do either," Leon said turning to me.

This was going downhill fast and I was afraid of what Leon might want to get off of his chest. Fortunately Freddy thought the same.

"You are in a mood, aren't you? I know just what you need," said Freddy as he proceeded to fix Leon a drink.

That was exactly the opposite of what Leon needed. But I knew that it was time for me withdraw from this conversation because I would only make things worse.

The party that night was lovely. The food was incredible and I could only imagine what Freddy must have spent on catering. He had a full bar with a bartender on the terrace and two really cute waiters walking around with trays of delectables. I estimated around eighty well-dressed guests in attendance, of which two-thirds were men. Martin and Marc were there and Marc had greeted me with a full-frontal kiss on the lips. From the corner of my eye, I saw Freddy smirk.

Leon's earlier cocktail had turned into another and another so that by the time the party had started, he was already on his way to being drunk. What worried me most was wondering what secrets he might reveal. Liquor had a way of eliminating all of Leon's filters.

When I noticed Leon leaning against a pedestal that held a bronze sculpture, I moved quickly in his direction wanting to catch him before he stumbled and knocked it over. Just as I reached Leon and secured the collectable from the other side, some pompous queen walked over dressed in seersucker shorts, a pink polo shirt, with a lime green sweater draped across his shoulders. He was considerably older than most of the guests and I thought trying a little too hard to pull off the current "preppy" fashion trend.

"I'm surprised to see you here," he said to Leon. "Of course, I was more surprised that they let you out of the slammer."

I was caught off guard and quickly tried to figure out what to do as Leon looked at him and slurred a rousing string of profanities. Fortunately, Freddy had made his way over by then and looked his arrogant guest directly in the face.

"Back off, Earl. Peddle your drama at someone else's party," Freddy said sternly.

With that Earl, nodded and backed away. Leon had already forgotten the encounter.

"What was that all about and should I be concerned?" I asked Freddy.

"You know what Leon was arrested for?" he asked.

I nodded.

"That was who he worked for at the time," he said.

"And you thought it would be wise to bring them together at your party?" I asked our host.

"Clearly not my smartest move," Freddy replied with a knowing laugh.

I guided Leon to a chair and gave him a slight shove backward. He had moved into the sloppy drunk stage and Freddy's home had way too many breakables that might not survive the night if Leon was free to roam.

Marc came over and asked if I was alright.

"Yes, thank you. It has been an enlightening evening so far," I said sarcastically.

"Anything that I can do to take your mind off of things?" Marc offered.

So tempting and so dangerous. I wondered which would win out. I was flattered and also attracted to Marc. And Leon, well, Leon had been a prick all day and it had felt like he was pushing me away.

"How about just another drink for now?" I relented.

"I am on it," said Marc as he made his way over to the bartender before I could tell him what I wanted. He returned with a scotch and water and handed it to me.

"How did you know?" I asked surprised.

"I've been watching you," Marc replied.

"Like a stalker?" I asked with a grin.

"If that turns you on," Marc suggestively said.

Oh my, it did but I could not let this go any further. Or could I?

—●—

The next morning we packed our bags, said our goodbyes to Freddy and the other guests, and began our journey home. The ride back seemed twice as long as the ride to the party. Leon had not spoken two words to me for miles and miles.

"Do you want to stop and get something to eat?" I asked.

"I don't care but we are going to need gas soon," Leon replied. And with that, he pulled off at the next exit and put gas in his car. There was a fast food restaurant across the street.

"Is that okay?" Leon asked pointing.

"Sure, it's fine," I replied.

We went through the drive-through and then got back on the interstate. As I had done in the past, I unwrapped his burger and handed it to him. I then emptied a couple of ketchup packets onto the wrapper for his fries.

"Thanks," he said.

We rode a while longer in silence as Leon looked straight ahead.

"I think I need to move out," said Leon.

I felt blindsided. I knew we had problems. His drinking. My bitching. But I kept thinking we would work that out.

"What brought that on?" I asked.

"You're not happy and I'm not happy," he replied.

"Is there anything that I can do to make you happy? To make this better?" I asked knowing that I could not deny his assessment.

"No. I don't think so," he said.

I felt tears begin to well up in my eyes but I did not want to cry. I had known deep down that it was not working but never had the nerve to address the issue. Still it hurt, much more than I would have thought. One, losing him and two, feeling like I had failed.

"Don't blame yourself," he said. "I know that you are. We have both messed up and I think it's just too far gone to fix."

"Does Freddy know?" I asked him.

"Yes, I talked it over with him," he answered coolly.

"I did not even know that the two of you were that close. I can't remember when you ever talked about him or called him or anything. But now he is your confidant?" I said.

"I did talk about him. You just never listened. And I called him two or three times a week from work. We have that 800 number there that I can use," he explained.

Just one more thing that I never knew about him. *Was he keeping secrets or did I really not bother to listen or ask questions? Did I just not care about anything in his life?*

"When?" I asked.

"When am I moving out?"

"Yes"

"Soon. I think that I have found a place," he said matter-of-factly.

"You've already been looking? You've been planning this for a while?" I continued.

"Yes. Sorry."

How had I not picked up on this? Was I so much in my own little world that I was ignorant to everything going on around me?

"Does anyone else know?" I asked.

"You mean, your friends?"

"They are your friends, too," I said.

"Whatever, no. The only person I mentioned it to is someone I work with – he has been helping me look for something," he answered.

"Are you having an affair with someone from work?" I asked, not sure I really wanted to know.

"No, there isn't anyone else," he said and I believed him. He then looked over at me.

"Did you do anything with Marc over the weekend?"

"No. He wanted to and I will admit that I was tempted. But I could not follow through.

What about you?" I replied.

"Did I mess around with someone?" he asked.

"Yes," I said.

"No."

—•—

"You are making that up," Bill said in disbelief.

"No, I'm not," I said.

"Surely you can work it out," said Dan.

"He's kidding," Bill said butting in.

"No, Bill. I'm not, and Dan, he does not want to work it out," I said. "I'm not even sure that we could if we tried."

"You really aren't kidding?" Bill asked.

"Oh. My. God. Bill," Dan said. "Give it a rest. Leon is leaving Ricky. Now you are up to speed."

"I never thought it would last," Bill said, trying to look offended.

"For once in your life, Bill, shut up," yelled Greg. "Just shut up and listen. You sound like your sister."

"Are you okay?" Greg asked, turning to me.

"I don't know. There is a part of me that is relieved and a part of me that is so sad," I answered.

I had asked Bill, Dan, Greg and Dean to meet me for dinner. Dean said that he had a date but the others were happy to join me, especially since I said that I was paying.

"Has he found a place?" Dan asked.

"I think so. He is planning on being out by the weekend."

"That fast?" Greg asked.

"Yes."

Bill finally asked the question that I had been expecting to come up.

"What about your stuff? Your furniture and all? What does he want? How much does he want?"

Dan and Greg both looked at Bill, wanting to reprimand him but at the same time dying of curiosity as well. All three of them turned to me.

"We haven't officially divided everything. He did say that he did not expect anything that I owned before he moved in. However, he did think that half of everything we collected since he moved in should be his," I answered.

"Wow. I never thought about what would happen in a breakup," said Greg. "That's a lot to lose."

"True. But it's fair," I replied. "I can't argue with him. He did help steal what he is asking for. The bad thing is that I have gotten attached to some of those things. But now we both will have to make concessions. We both will have to give up things we like just to keep things that we love."

"Do you know what you want?" asked Bill.

"Bill, seriously, he just told us he breaking up and you are already worried about what he gets to keep," Dan said in a huff.

"It's okay. I have thought about it and I need to think about it. I need to have a game plan," I replied. "But when it comes down to it, I may want this or that but will have to give up one or the other. I need this breakup to be as friendly as possible.

None of us needs an irate and vindictive Leon."

"The one thing that you can count on keeping in the breakup," said Greg. "The three of us, and Dean, whether you want him or not. We are Team Ricky, or should I say Team Nathaniel?"

All three of my dear friends then gathered around for a group hug and the tears that I had held back for so long began to flow.

—●—

Leon moved into a small rental house in an up-and-coming neighborhood. He wanted to show it to me so that I could offer ideas for paint colors and suggestions for furniture placement. We had taken turns one night dividing the pieces that had been acquired after Leon had moved in. We then went to our storage unit and continued until a decision was made on everything. I did lose a few things that I had hoped to keep. Of course the pieces that had been in storage never really felt like mine in the first place, since I had not yet had the opportunity to live with them. However, I would be able to bring several of those remaining pieces over to fill in the empty spots left by Leon.

I really fought for the Roman statues on each side of the fireplace. However, when I saw just how much he wanted them, I suggested that we break up the pair and each keep one.

"Fine, then I will take the antique lowboy," said Leon.

"I had the lowboy before you moved in," I said. "So, no."

I thought about the statues and decided that it just was not worth the fight.

"You can have them," I relented. "They should stay together."

Once everything was in his new place, he still had room for more and was ready to fill it up. I had never found dining room furniture for Greg and now Leon was making a list of things he felt that he should have. Just my luck, he wanted dining room furniture, too.

—●—

"Leon wants me to help him find things to furnish his new house," I shared with Bill and Dan.

"You are kidding, aren't you? He just cleaned you out and he still wants more?" said Bill.

"He did not clean me out, he just made a dent. A serious dent and yet somehow, I am still left with a pretty full house," I replied.

"I say no. Let him get his own stuff. He is no longer a part of the midnight crew. He lost that right when he moved out," Bill said adamantly.

"You do not really have a say in what Ricky does, Bill. Neither do I," Dan said, letting his frustration with Bill show.

"Look, you do not have to help. I don't even know of a place right now to hit. It is getting harder and harder to find anything. And when I do, they have so much security in place that I am scared to even look," I said.

"How does Greg feel about it?" Bill asked.

"He still wants dining room furniture. He and Dean ended up moving their patio furniture inside just to have a table where they can eat," I said.

"Sounds like you need to find a big-ass mess of furniture somewhere so that we can all go on one last run," Dan said.

"One last run?" Bill asked in disbelief.

— ● —

Leon called me and acted very sweet and concerned. Then he got to the point of his call — had I found anything?

"You don't have to fake being interested in my life. Just go ahead and ask," I said. "You want to know why I haven't found any furniture yet, right?"

"You don't have to be pissy. I am trying to be nice," Leon replied. "But yes, when are you going to find something? Or am I going to have to do it myself?"

"That would be a bad idea, Leon. You are careless and you would get caught," I warned.

"Like you almost did getting that patio furniture for Greg? Yes, Dean let it slip one night how the cops showed up. I told you to be careful, but no, you think you are bulletproof," Leon said with an "I told you so" tone.

"Well, I have never been to prison," I replied.

I knew that I had gone too far by the silence on the other end of the line.

"I am looking Leon, and I will find something soon," I added quickly.

—•—

I heard through the gossip mill that Leon was out in the bars nightly, often plastered and needing a cab home. However, one night he thought that he was sober enough to drive and ended up running his car off the side of the road. He was not far from his home and by some miracle he was able to walk there before the police showed up. Other than his car, there was no other property damage. The police knocked on his door the next morning but by then he was sober enough and they did not have a reason to suspect otherwise. Leon told them that a dog ran into the street in front of his car and that he had swerved to miss it. I don't know if they bought his lie but he came out of it with only a few bumps and bruises. However, the passenger side of his car was damaged from bumper to bumper. He had insurance but of course his premium escalated after he turned in the claim.

Between his rent and utilities, along with the nightly booze fests, money was tight for Leon. So he came up with a harebrained idea to stage a break-in and collect on his contents insurance policy.

None of us knew anything about his scheme until he called Bill and Dan one night and said that his house had been broken into. They immediately called me and the three of us rushed over. Leon had yet to notify the cops and that was a good thing. Yes, there was a broken window but Bill took one look at it and then looked at Leon with disgust.

"If you are going to call the cops, you might want to clean up the glass outside and bring it inside because – now correct me if I am wrong – wouldn't a thief break the window from the outside causing the broken glass to be inside?" Bill ranted. "But you, you dumb ass, you broke your own window from the inside. No cop is going to buy your story and then no insurance company will either. They are going to smell fraud, big time. Plus, you don't have a receipt for anything that you own."

Leon looked like he had been slapped across the face, and Lord knows, someone should have done that. What an idiot.

"Please help me. I'm broke. I can't pay my bills," Leon said looking at Bill, then Dan and then me.

"Let's get the glass cleaned up," I said. "Do you have any gloves?"

Leon never admitted to breaking the window himself but it was so clear that it was exactly what he had done. The three of us played along to save him more embarrassment.

"What was stolen?" asked Bill.

"A painting, a pair of candlesticks and..." Leon hesitated.

"What else?" I asked, knowing it had to be something big.

"The pair of Roman statues," he said.

All three of us stopped what we were doing. I could not believe that I had not immediately noticed them missing from beside his fireplace. I felt like knocking Leon upside his head.

"You mean, out of everything in here, you are telling us that someone broke through your window and took two of the heaviest things that you own?" I yelled.

"Yes," Leon answered defiantly.

Bill looked at me and shook his head.

"Let's go," he said.

"We are almost done," Dan said. "Finish up and then we can go."

We had most of the glass out of the yard and dropped inside on the floor in his living room in front of the broken window. Bill and Dan started toward the door.

"Good luck," said Dan.

Bill did not have anything else to say to Leon. He was furious and understandably so.

"Please be careful," I said looking at Leon. "This is a dangerous game that you are playing."

Chapter Eighteen
present day

The second day of the sale began at the hour advertised. My understanding is on the second, or last day, it is a different crowd – the serious bargain hunters. They assume that the sale is about to end and that you are so desperate to get rid of everything that you will practically give it away. Well, I am not desperate.

"How did you sleep?" asked Roberta Ann. "I hope you got some rest. And let me just say again, we can handle this if you would rather not be here."

"No, I am good. I want to see this through to the end. Let the games begin!"

I immediately noticed that today's crowd moved at a more leisurely pace. They probably thought it was already picked over from yesterday so there was no need to hurry. I plopped myself back down in my lawn chair and people-watched. I thought back to the days when everyone would dress up. Of course, I did not expect coat and ties but seriously, some of these clowns looked like they were still in their pajamas. I wanted to get a notepad and pen and issue fashion citations. Or hold up scorecards like they do at sporting events and grade everyone with a number. I was getting myself tickled just thinking about it when I looked up and saw Bill walking my way with the assistance of a cane.

"What are doing here, you old goat?" I said.

"I saw the ad online about your sale," he said smiling. "I had to see if there was anything that I needed."

"You don't need a thing and you know it. You're just being nosey. But it is so good to see you anyway. It has been way too long," I said.

Bill and I had reached the point of talking every few days but we had not physically gotten together in a few months. He had gone through a hip replacement and physical therapy and really did not want to be around anyone. But it looked like he was doing much better.

"You okay?" I asked.

"Why wouldn't I be?" he replied.

"Good Lord Bill, you did turn into your mean-as-a-snake sister. Don't be so testy. I did not mean anything by it. Just wondered how the new hip was doing."

"Sorry, it is so much better but I hate the physical therapy. Except the other day, my usual therapist was out and this strapping young stud was her replacement. Speaking of pain and pleasure. He was so easy on the eyes," Bill said with a devilish grin.

"And I am sure that he was young enough to be your great-grandson."

"I see you haven't gotten any less bitchy in your old age," he said as he tried to keep from laughing.

"It is an art form," I proudly responded.

"So what's with the sale? I figured that you would ask to be buried with your possessions and your tombstone would read 'Here lies Nathaniel – his final midnight run.' Sound about right?"

"You are still not as clever as you think you are." I said. "It was time. I knew I needed out of this big house. And definitely I need to give up climbing stairs."

"Just when are you going to have that knee replacement?" Bill asked.

Ignoring him, I continued. "And if I am moving, downsizing, why have all this clutter? I want something shiny and new."

"Are you talking about men or your furnishings?" Bill asked.

"You are a lecherous old fart, aren't you?

"You used to like that about me," he said playfully.

"Anyway, as I was saying, I am moving into the retirement place down the street. I will have a new two bedroom apartment with meals included. I can even ride the elevator and not have to deal with stairs. Why don't you join me?" I asked sincerely.

"I should, but I can't give up everything. I already had to give up enough when Dan left me."

"Really, Bill, that was what twenty, twenty-five years ago? Are you still holding a grudge? He earned what he took. Either from the hard work involved with stealing it, or having to work with you in that miserable catering business, or dealing with your family all of those years. In fact, you probably should have given him your half as well."

"He still shouldn't have left," Bill said reminiscing about the good old days.

"I know, but people change. You were together at least fifteen years. And it is not like you were lonely for long after he moved out."

Bill glanced over at my antique chest of drawers and then heaved himself up out of the chair to take a closer look. One of the younger salesladies rushed over and offered to help.

"If you would like to know anything about this chest, that gentleman over there is full of stories," she offered, pointing in my direction.

"Ricky," she yelled. "This man is interested in your antique chest. Why don't you tell him about it."

"I keep telling you, I am not deaf and that old perv is not going to buy anything," I snapped.

She looked horrified and started to apologize to Bill.

"He's right and for the record, I was there when he picked it up. But I agree that he's full of something and trust me, I know the story. In fact, I know all of the stories."

That certainly got her attention.

"Bill, behave. Remember I have stories of my own."

I motioned for Bill to follow me inside to the kitchen where I made us each a cup of coffee. The kitchen, bathrooms and my bedroom were off limits during the sale so it gave us a little bit of privacy.

"Still want cream?" I asked, although I knew the answer.

"Yes. Lots."

"I know. We used to say 'Bill likes a little coffee with his cream.'"

"Wasn't funny then and hasn't gotten any funnier with age," he said, trying to act mad.

"So what are you doing these days to amuse yourself?"

Bill had sold his catering business a few years ago for a good profit. There was a time that he had tried his hand at owning a restaurant, but there was just too much competition and keeping help was always a problem. He about lost his shirt over that venture, then rebounded by building up the catering biz to the point that it was profitable enough that someone was willing to pay him for it.

"Not much. I thought about buying another house and fixing it up. But I'm not sure that I have it in me," he said.

Over the last several years, after Dan moved out, Bill had bought, remodeled and sold five houses. It gave him something to do – plus I think that he also liked having the assortment of construction workers around. He has had that hard-hat fantasy for as long as I can remember – all the way back to the late 1970s and the Village People. Personally, my favorite in the group was always the cowboy.

"I do still look at real estate and every once in a while, I will see something in a model that I think might be easy to take. But honestly, I just don't have the energy anymore," said Bill.

"Well, everyone now has an alarm system or security cameras. Neighbors are watching out with their cell phone cameras ready to catch you in the act. It's all too risky now. But back in the 1970s and 1980s, we sure did have a good run," I commented.

"Have you ever thought about – I mean, sat there and really thought about everything that we did? I don't have a clue just how much we picked up over the years. I surely don't remember everything you or Greg got. Hell, I don't even remember everything that I ended up with. There were things that I got rid of as soon as something better came along. I do have a few party pics from long ago and I will see something in a photo that I no longer own and had totally forgotten about. We could have furnished a dozen houses easily."

"It is overwhelming," I said. "And even though I am selling off a bunch of my stuff, there are a couple of things that I am going to hold on to just for old times sake."

"I hear ya. I will never get rid of that desk from the interior design studio. I love it just as much today as I did way back then. Speaking of which, we never did find out if he actually lived there or just how close we came that night to being caught."

"I thought I told you," I said. "Wait a second, let me see if I can recall. I did hear something later on and I am thinking it was that he did live there. That's right, the story was that he could not afford to have a design studio and a home, so he combined them and lived in that back room. Oh yes, I remember now, what I heard was there was a time that he had forgotten to lock the front door and a customer came in one day while he was in the back doing the nasty with the bug guy. You know, the exterminator. What I heard was, they were so into it that they did not hear the front door open. But the client heard a noise, thought someone was being attacked, and opened the bedroom door only to find legs and arms all tangled up and him looking just like a dead cockroach on his back."

"You are making that up."

"No, that client was so disgusted that they hired another designer, someone that I knew. They told him all about it."

"It is still a miracle that we did not break in and find him ourselves or that he did not come home and catch us," said Bill.

"That could be said about every one of our nightly adventures. I would like to say that we weren't caught because we were living right, but we both know that would be a big ol' lie."

At that point Bill wanted to get serious. He wanted to know why I was moving. If I was dying. Because that was the only reason he could think of to make me want to sell off everything.

"I promise, I am not dying," I assured him. "Well, at least not today. I am just tired. It is lonely in this big house and the upkeep is ridiculous. I don't feel like doing any of the work myself but I also don't feel like having anyone around either. I let go of the cleaning crew a few months ago. It was one of those services and each week it seemed like somebody new was coming into my home. Not only would I have to explain everything again and again, but things kept getting broken. Of course the problem now is that I don't want to clean it myself – so what do I do?"

"Well, you don't walk away and give up."

"I am not giving up. Don't you ever get tired of everything? Yes, my home was gorgeous but it just felt like it was too much. It has always felt like too much. I mean I paid for a storage unit for years and even had to move up to a larger unit at one point before I bought this house. And why did I really want this house? Because I needed a place for all of my stuff. It would have been easier to have gotten rid of some of my beautiful junk."

"You did sell off things every once in a while," Bill reminded me.

"True, I would have a client who came into my home and then said that they liked something and then convinced me to sell it to them. So I did."

"You know that was every bit as risky as having the newspaper photograph our homes," he said. "At least, with the paper you would have been able to control what was in a photo. But, once you have sold an item, you would have no idea if the client would throw a big party or have their home in some publication. And it could all lead back to someone asking where something came from."

"We've had this discussion before," I said. "You don't think that I never thought of that?"

"I'm not scolding you," he said. "Even if you and I were very careful, we lost what control we might have had when Leon and Dan moved out. Of course, now it has been so long that I can't imagine there would be a problem."

"And that's why I feel comfortable having a public sale now. So much time has past," I added. "And as far as Leon goes, I'm not sure that I ever had control over him in the first place. I could not compete with the alcohol."

"Leon was a handful. And I'm not saying that I told you so, but it was clear that he had a drinking problem from the start and that doesn't always get better," Bill said. "And you knew it but did not want to accept it. Or stupidly thought that you could change him. Do you ever think about him or miss him? I mean, you never allowed yourself to get in another relationship even though there were plenty of guys who were interested."

"First of all, I have way too many secrets to ever get involved with anyone else. And as far as Leon goes, I think about him now and again? Sure. Miss him? Rarely. That was more than thirty years ago."

"I know I haven't asked you about him in a quite a while, but when was the last time that you heard from him? Is he even still alive?" Bill asked.

"I assume so, although I haven't had contact with him in a good five years or more. Why are you dredging this up now, Bill?" I asked. "Yes, deep down I knew he was an alcoholic. When we were at the beach I kept telling myself that he is on vacation and just having fun. Loosening up. Plus, he was so damn cute."

"I can't argue with you there," Bill conceded. "And a sweetheart when he was sober. And I really do think he was crazy about you for a while."

"Remember the break-in?" he added after a minute.

"Which one? We did so many?" I asked.

"Not one of ours," Bill explained. "Leon's break-in. You

know, the one where the window was clearly broken from the inside like someone was trying to get out?"

"He was so pitiful. And even after being caught in a lie, he continued to try and convince us otherwise. I got so mad that I just had to walk away."

"Did you suspect right away that Freddy was involved?" Bill asked.

"No. But as soon as he said the Roman statues had been stolen, I knew."

"That was the funniest thing, when you asked Dan and me to come back to your place because you suspected something," he continued. "We did not know what you thought had happened. But we were dying of curiosity."

"The look on both of your faces was priceless when I picked up the phone and dialed. You looked so confused until I said 'Hello Freddy, is Leon there yet?' And remember, he said, 'No, I think he's on his way.' He did not have a clue that he was being played."

"I know," said Bill laughing. "Then you asked him if Leon was bringing the statues and stuff with him."

"And he said, 'Yeah' that he had made him a deal too good to pass up," I added.

"Unbelievable. Leon staged a break-in to collect insurance and then sold the stolen goods to Freddy."

"Twice stolen," I said, correcting Bill.

"Right, twice stolen. I would have loved to have seen

Leon's face when Freddy relayed your conversation. Because you know that he did," said Bill.

"I imagine so but Leon never brought it up, did he? Still, that did not stop him from expecting me to help him get more furniture," I said.

"I know. And you did. Hell, we all did," Bill concluded.

Chapter Nineteen

It was now the mid 1980s and I had been working steadily in the design business for several years. I had finally achieved the enviable position of repeat customers. And I steadily picked up new clients from referrals. My interior design business was flourishing. This allowed me to work for clients who had homes in town as well as clients with second homes either at the beach or in the mountains.

I even had a design job back in the same beachside town where Leon and I first met.

I arrived three days ahead of my client to have things ready for them in advance. There was a lot to do but I had to face the fact that all work and no play made me stir crazy. I decided to take one afternoon off and have some fun. My first thought was to go to a movie but on the way to the theater, I passed a sign with an arrow to turn left, then right to *Check out the furnished models* at a new development on the bay side.

The building was designed so that you had to pass through the office before being directed to the three furnished model units – a one bedroom, a two bedroom and a three bedroom. The first level of the building was covered parking with the office and models on the second floor.

I felt a tinge of anticipation as I pulled into a parking place. My love of design was still strong and my mind was anxious with curiosity. I loved finding inspiration in others' work – and I had been known to even "borrow" an idea or two. I also enjoyed playing a made-up game of "what if?" What if I were there to steal? What would I be most interested in and how would I get away with it?

The agent on duty appeared to be preoccupied. She said for me to take a look and then let her know if I had any questions. Even though I had no plans to steal anything, my years of training caused me to focus on and analyze the situation. Right off, I knew that the second floor was a problem because you would have to deal with the elevator or stairway when making a getaway. The units also opened onto a common hallway, and at any moment someone could come out of their condo or simply peer through their front door peephole and have a fisheye view of the hall. I did notice that even though they expected you to exit through the office, you could actually avoid it. That was the only positive that I was able to come up with so far. Of course, I thought smaller items could be dropped from the balcony to someone below, but that had disaster written all over it.

The models were attractive and as expected, decorated in beachy colors and furnishings. Seafoam green, soft blues and mauve tones dominated two of the units. The designer went bold in the three-bedroom model with yellow, orange and tomato red. It was very striking but not at all calming for a relaxing getaway – I felt that I would grow tired of those colors in short order. Walking through the models, I let myself imagine what I might take and where I would use them. In reality, only a few accessories would fit with my current decor back home.

In the two-bedroom unit's master suite, there was a wooden lighthouse sitting on the dresser that I would have sworn was identical to the one Leon and I had stolen several years earlier from a similar beach home. It made me smile and remember the good times that we had shared before it all went to hell.

As much as I enjoyed my afternoon break, I knew that I did not need to steal anything and I did not really want anything that I saw. Plus, I most definitely was aware of how unsafe it would be. Just not worth the effort.

As soon I got back home from my trip I had a call from Greg, followed by a call from Leon. Both were curious if I had located dining room furniture for them – and basically, if not, why not.

Feeling pressured, I decided that I needed to expand my search. The counties to the north and south of town were growing and new options were springing up here and there. Again, some of the ones that I saw were too perilous. They either had alarm systems or security patrolling the neighborhoods. I was not foolish enough to think that it was all for my benefit. I imagined that there were other thieves out there muscling in on our territory. I had certainly heard about construction sites where building materials, appliances and yes, even lighting fixtures had been stolen. Been there. Done that. Even left one on the side of the road.

New developments with furnished models also had construction going on. The security patrols' first priority might have been to keep building materials from disappearing, but it was also keeping me from wanting to plan any kind of hit on their model.

South of town in a neighboring county, a brand new golf course community was breaking ground. They already had their clubhouse as well as the golf course in place. There were a half dozen homes that looked finished and lived in and ten or more houses in some stage of construction.

Plus, they had a furnished model and not just any furnished model. It was a four-bedroom, one-story home with three baths, living room, dining room, kitchen with breakfast area, and even a bonus room over the garage. I toured the home during a Sunday afternoon open house and saw no signs of an alarm. There were several people looking at the model at the same time, so it was easy enough for me to open closet doors and investigate without attracting attention. Without an alarm, I wondered if they thought that maybe they were safe because they were not in the big city. Less than two miles away sat Creekview, the condominium development where Greg and I, one morning (with a car load including my velvet sofa) got pulled over by the county police.

I did not tell my posse about my find. I needed to be sure that it was even a possibility before getting their hopes up. I drove back out there several nights in a row to check but never saw any signs of a security patrol. It appeared almost too good to be true. *Were they just bating someone to rob them so that they could catch them?* I rationalized that most likely, they had plans to add security but had foolishly opted to wait.

This was another situation when I thought that late afternoon might be best. It was so isolated and dark at night that a car along with a van at the model home would immediately raise suspicion for the few folks who lived there – or the police, if they drove through to check. I also knew that if it was too early in the day, construction crews would still be around and if they saw something out of the norm they might become concerned.

Bill, Dan and I still had flexible hours while Greg, Leon and Dean worked until five. Sundown was around 6:30 at that time of year and the house was a twenty-minute drive from my home. I needed to have a plan in place before I talked with any of the guys. One or two opinions would be bad enough – however, six opinions could mean nothing would be decided. I started with Bill and Dan, as I trusted their instincts more than any of the others.

"It's a shame that we have to involve the three stooges," Bill said. "This would be a sweet job just for us."

"It's not happening, Bill. I have to uphold my commitment to Greg. This model has a breakfast room table and chairs that I know that he would like," I said. "And I also feel that I need to help Leon, hopefully for the last time. I don't want to renege on him about the dining room furniture and again, this house has that as well. The three of us do not need anything so whatever we come away with will be a bonus."

"And Dean? Do you feel an obligation to him too?" asked Dan.

"No, he is not part of the equation other than the connection to Greg. Dean hasn't asked for anything and I do not feel that I owe him anything," I replied.

"So what's the plan?" asked Bill.

"Okay, see if this makes any sense. I think that if all six of us descend on this home in four or five cars and then start arguing about who is getting what – well, we might as well turn ourselves in right now," I said.

"Agreed," Bill and Dan said in unison.

"I feel that the three of us should go first, select a few things and load them up. Then I will call Greg to come get his table and chairs, followed by calling Leon to do the same," I continued.

"Are you thinking that we stay and help them or just get our stuff and go — let them take care of getting their own?" asked Bill.

"As much as I would like to do it that way, I think that we need to stay and help just to make sure they get in and out without getting caught," I responded.

I went on to explain that I never did find a key and that the windows had storm windows. This complicated things, as we could not simply raise a window and crawl through. And while there was a sliding glass door on the back, I had noticed a broom handle wedged at the bottom to make sure that you could not open it.

"I have been seeing that trick more and more," I explained and then continued. "There are two garage doors in back but we would need to come in another way, then unhook one to load out. There is a pair of doors in the front and you know they usually give way with very little effort. So, I am thinking that we will have to go through the front."

"Then what?" asked Bill.

"We'll take your van and my car and fill them with whatever you want other than the two dining sets. Then we will call Greg and Leon once we have unloaded and are ready to go back. I will call tonight and tell each of them to leave tomorrow night free and wait for my call," I answered.

"I still think it stands a good chance of going south with six people involved," said Dan. "We will have to be very cautious, watchful and willing to run at a moment's notice."

"I understand. So are you in?" I asked. "This may be Nathaniel and the Midnight Mover's swan song."

"Don't say that. Don't ever say that. We will never retire!" said Bill.

—●—

I called Greg and told him that I had found a dining table with four chairs and thought that tomorrow night would work. I asked him to be ready, along with Dean, and to wait for my call. He was excited and wanted a description and I did my best to fill him in.

"What else is there?" Greg asked. "I wouldn't mind a few other things as well."

"Let's plan on the table and chairs. If there is time and we still feel good, then we'll deal with it. Okay?" I asked.

After Greg, I called Leon. He answered with a bit of attitude and I started to say, "Forget it" and hang up. But instead, I gave him the same rundown as Greg. I did not tell either of them about the other. There was no sense in getting each of them worked up thinking that they would have to fight over things. Like Greg, Leon wanted a description and was pleased to hear the dining table would seat six.

"How are we going to be able to move it? Will it even fit in your car?" inquired Leon.

"I have asked Bill to help with his van," I answered.

"He doesn't mind?" asked Leon.

"You know Bill, he complained a bit," I said. "But he will help. Stay near your phone."

"Okay. And Ricky?" said Leon.

"Yes."

"Thank you. I mean it, thank you," he said endearingly.

There was that sweetness that I remembered from when we first met.

The next afternoon, Bill and Dan met me at a nearby shopping center where we parked their van. They rode with me over to the subdivision where we circled the neighborhood to make sure it still looked safe. I pulled my car into the drive in front of the model home. The three of us jumped out and walked around the house to double check that nothing had been left unlocked or a key hidden. We agreed that the front doors would be our best option.

Without homes across the street, Bill felt comfortable bumping the doors, again and again. This pair of solid wood doors was clearly bolted and stubborn but finally opened wide. However, one door split and would not close properly once we were inside. I quickly slid a dining chair over to hold it in place.

"Go," I said after taking a deep breath.

I already knew what was available from my previous trip, but the boys needed a moment to take a quick look to see what they might want.

"You found it, so you go first and tell us what you would like," offered Bill after they had made a tour of the rooms.

I said that I liked the chair in the master bedroom and the tea cart in the dining room. I then asked Bill and Dan what they wanted while I continued to observe the front yard from the dining room window. They both ticked off their list and we all agreed that everything should be able to fit in our vehicles in one trip. Dan offered to stay at the house and move what he could toward the garage while Bill and I went back to retrieve his van. I told Dan to be constantly checking the front to make sure that no one snuck up on him. It made me nervous leaving him alone.

"We will be quick," Bill said as he gave Dan a quick smooch.

Off we went. We were probably only gone about ten minutes but to me, it felt like it was taking forever. After having that experience of returning to the crime scene to find flashing blue lights waiting, I held my breath when I turned onto the street. Fortunately, everything looked the same.

Bill pulled his van around back and I parked in front. I had already mentioned that I thought it might be the smartest thing because anyone passing by would hopefully think it was the realtor. However, a van parked in front with furniture being loaded would make a completely different first impression.

I casually walked around back, not wanting to attract attention, then immediately jumped in helping the boys load – before remembering that I should be on lookout. I went back to the front window and waited.

"The van is loaded but we still have three or four more things. Do you want to go ahead and move your car?" Bill said breaking the silence.

"No, let me watch. You move it, please," I asked as I handed Bill my car keys.

From my spot in the dining room, I saw Bill get into my car and then watched as it disappeared around the corner of the house. He and Dan quickly loaded the remaining items.

"There is still a little room," said Bill.

"Okay, let's each grab something, throw it in and go," I instructed.

About twenty-five minutes later, we were back at my condo and unloading into my garage. I called Greg and told him to meet us at the same shopping center where we had parked Bill's van earlier. He knew where it was and nearly thirty minutes later met us there with Dean riding in the passenger seat. Opting to leave my car at home, Bill, Dan and I rode in the van. The sole purpose of this trip was to grab the dining set and whatever else he might want, within reason.

Greg followed us to the house and then parked around back. I opened the garage door.

"This way," I said. All of a sudden it sank in to Greg and Dean that we had already been there.

"You've hit it already? Without us?" Greg said in a huff.

"Yes, and if you want to get mad, do it later," I said. "Unless you don't want the table and chairs."

I could tell he was torn but the furniture won out. With five of us loading, we had it in the van in a heartbeat.

"I am going to watch the front and you grab whatever else you want and then we need to go," I added.

Out of nowhere a car came slowly down the street.

"Car," I yelled.

Everyone stopped in their tracks. Greg and Dean were in the kitchen and Bill was closest to me in the dining room taking pictures down off the wall. Dan rushed in and stood next to me. The car turned into the drive and came to a stop in front. A young couple with a small child got out and began walking down the sidewalk toward the broken front door. Bill and Dan were starting to panic and Dean had gone pale.

"We need run, now," insisted Bill.

I was about to agree and then I saw Greg step into the dining room.

"Ricky's got this," he said. "Just wait, you'll see – it will be fine."

I opened the busted front door, stepped onto the porch and took a deep breath.

"Hello, may I help you?"

"Is the model open?" asked the husband.

"Normally it would be. But as you can see, we have had a break-in," I said, pointing to the busted door. "I'm Richard Stinger, the realtor. I just got here and now I'm waiting for the police. Since it is a crime scene, I really can't let you come in."

"Oh, I see, they really made a mess of the door. Did they also do damage inside?" asked the wife with concern.

"No, but they did get away with quite a lot of our furnishings. I hope that you understand," I said adding, "Please come back another day. It really is a lovely home."

Behind me, I knew the four of them were frozen like mannequins and imagining that almost got me tickled. However, I held my composure as the young couple thanked me and said that they understood. The husband even offered for them to wait in their car until the police arrived just to make sure I was safe.

"Thank you, but I imagine that the thieves are long gone by now," I replied.

The young family drove away and I felt as if I was about to collapse.

"I told you," said Greg proudly. "Ricky can lie his way out of anything."

"Richard Stinger? Where did that name come from?" asked Bill.

"Richard is because of Ricky, right?" asked Dan.

"Yes."

"But what about Stinger?" Bill asked.

I started singing a little bit of my favorite song from a couple of years back, *Every Breath You Take* and then waited for it to sink in.

"Yes, we all know that you have a huge crush on Sting," said Greg.

"Sting. Stinger, right?" Dan added.

But it was Dean, who had been quiet during all of this, who put the pieces together.

"And Sting is in the band, The Police," Dean said with a knowing smile.

"Not funny. Not funny at all, Ricky," said Bill.

"Who has Kleenex, because I am about to have an accident?" asked Dan.

"We need to go, now," said Greg still laughing.

Wow. All of us had gotten so wrapped up discussing my performance that we had forgotten we were still standing in a crime scene with a loaded van and car.

We took everything back to Greg's apartment and helped them carry it upstairs.

"Some day you'll have to tell me what all of you took before you let us see the house," Greg said in a miffed tone.

"That was how I got them to help you. So, let it go, and tell them thanks," I whispered, knowing Bill and Dan were in the other room.

Greg and Dean did act sincerely grateful for our help. I hoped that would be the last time that I would hear anything about taking them on another midnight run.

Now, we still had Leon to deal with. I will admit that after the encounter with the young family, I was not feeling quite as adventuresome as earlier. I would have preferred not to go back.

"Do we have to go back?" Bill asked sensing my reservations.

"What choice do we have? I have to help him and I need your van to do so. Do you want to let me borrow it or come along and help?" I asked.

"We will help. Call Leon," instructed Dan.

Leon was in a fairly good mood when I called and did not appear to be drunk. It was closer for him to meet at my home so I told him to come over and that Bill and Dan were already here with their van to help. He must have flown out of the door because it almost felt like he knocked on my front door about the same time that I hung up the phone.

"Ready?" I asked looking directly at Leon.

"Yes, what's the plan?" he asked eagerly.

"There is a dining table and six chairs with your name on it and anything else that you can fit in the van. And then we are done," Bill said.

I think Leon thought Bill meant done with that run. But I knew what Bill was really saying was that we were done with Leon after tonight. No more drama.

I rode with Bill and Dan rode with Leon. As we approached the house, I saw something that made me catch my breath.

"Wait, it looks like there is a car around back," I said to Bill.

"Shit," was all that he said.

But then I realized that it wasn't just any car, it was Greg's car. He and Dean had come back to get more.

And that was when I considered murder. I was livid. Bill pulled the van off to the side of the road and I jumped out and ran back to Leon's car. Dan already had his window down.

"What's up?" he asked.

"We have got company," I replied. But before he could panic, I added "It's Greg."

"What the hell? Why is he here, Ricky?" yelled Leon.

"Too long to explain. Do you want the table and chairs or not?" I asked matter-of-factly.

"Yes," answered Leon through gritted teeth.

"Then follow us," I instructed.

We pulled our vehicles around back, making it look like a used car lot. I got out and walked into the garage. I did not see anyone so I stepped into the kitchen, where Dean stood with a drapery rod in his hand ready to swat me.

"What are you doing here?" asked Dean.

"I could ask you the same thing. Are you idiots?" I replied. With that Greg stepped out from the other room where he had been hiding. I added, "I can't believe that you came back."

"Well, you came back. Hell, you even came out before you brought us here," Greg said with attitude.

"Dammit, I am just trying to keep everyone happy," I pleaded. "I promised Leon the dining room furniture. And before you get bent out of shape, you would not have room for it anyway. I brought everyone separately because I knew that it was way too risky. The cops will probably surround this place as six of us in three vehicles bicker over everything. Hell, they could be out there right now. If we get away with this, then I am done. No more. Do not even ask."

"Can we get my table and chairs and get out of here?" asked Leon.

"That the smartest thing I've heard all night," said Bill.

"Grab a chair and take it to the van. Now!" I said to Greg and Dean in a tone that made them jump. They did as they were told while Leon and Bill took the table to the garage. Once Leon's dining set was loaded, I looked at everyone and explained.

"It has gotten dark and we need to get away from here. Bill, Dan and I will go and take Leon's stuff. Seriously guys, it is not worth it. Please do not stay any longer," I begged. "Just grab one more thing and let's go."

"No," said Leon defiantly. "Each and every one of you got here before me and had your pick of everything. And now you are telling me that I can't even stay long enough to get my fair share?"

"There is no such thing as a fair share," I said. "It is what it is and right now, it is dangerous! We had a close call earlier with a family stopping by to look at the model. And now, it's dark and there are three cars in back. We have got to go!"

I then noticed that the front door was standing wide open. Of course, the dining chair that had held it closed was now in the van.

"Why is the front door open?" I screamed. "Should we just put a neon sign out front saying *Robbery in Progress?* You guys have totally lost it."

"What is that you want?" Bill asked Leon in a voice more calm than I am sure that he felt. "Tell us and let us help you get it loaded and then we need to go."

"We are out of here and no, we are not coming back," said Greg before Leon could answer. Looking at Bill and Dan, he added with fake sincerity, "Thank you for helping get the dinette set."

"What is it that you want?" I asked Leon as Greg and Dean drove away.

Leon haphazardly began pointing to things. A chair, a table, a lamp, this picture, that picture, that mirror.

"Okay, that's enough, Leon," Dan said. "All that is really left after these things are sofas, beds, that dresser and pool table. The remaining things are all too heavy, too big. Can we go now?"

Leon looked from side to side and then ran back into one of the bedrooms.

"Can we just shoot him?" asked Bill.

"I'm done," said Leon returning with a stack of throw pillows that had been on the master bedroom bed.

"Finally," Bill muttered and headed to his van.

"Help me grab the sofa and move it to hold the door shut," I said.

I was looking at Bill but Dan jumped in and helped me push. Once that was secure, we each picked up the pictures Leon had asked for and carried them to the van. I pulled down the garage door and joined Bill. Dan, once again, got into Leon's car. Slowly and carefully we drove to Leon's rental home and unloaded everything there.

Leon gave me a hug once we were done, and as much as I wanted to resist, I found myself relaxing into his arms. He kissed me and thanked me again. But I felt a finality that I had not felt with him before – not even during our breakup. I finally understood and accepted that this was it. We were done. It was time to move on with our lives.

Chapter Twenty

The following night, Dan, Bill and I divided our loot. There was no need to take turns. We had already asked for specific pieces while we were loading our vehicles at the model home. I looked around at everything and felt overwhelmed.

"Don't you feel like this is excessive? I mean, we do not need a thing and yet we keep stealing. Why?" I asked.

"Because it is there for the taking," said Bill being his usual smart-ass self.

"Wrong. It is because we are greedy," added Dan.

"I have never heard you complain about having a beautiful apartment to live in. You want it just as much as me," Bill said to Dan.

"I never asked for any of it. You just came in and filled every square inch," replied Dan.

"And that is why we are moving," countered Bill.

"Did they accept your offer?" I asked trying to steer the conversation in a safe direction.

"Yes, I think so. It's contingent on my credit report," said Bill.

"You know that will not be a problem with your catering business and such," I offered.

"He is buying it in his name because my credit, or lack of credit, might be a problem with the financing," added Dan.

"It is still our house even if it is in my name," said Bill wanting to make amends. "The apartment has been in your name all this time."

I had no idea that they had felt that way. They never talked about it in front of me, but now that I thought about it, it did look as if Dan was a kept man. Granted, they were in a relationship but Bill held the purse strings. Dan worked with him, but I am not sure if Bill gave Dan a paycheck or just an allowance. I could see how a bit of resentment might build up over time.

Surely, they will work it out and be fine. They have to be fine. Bill and Dan are one of the few things in my life that I truly felt I could count on.

We loaded their pieces into Bill's van and I asked if they had room in their apartment or if they were going to put them in storage.

"Storage, until we move," said Bill.

"I may start looking around for a house myself," I confided. "I have been thinking of getting something larger where I can work from home. I am tired of working out of someone else's showroom. It is time for me to stand on my own."

"You go, Miss Thing!" said Dan enthusiastically.

"Right back at ya!" I responded laughing.

—•—

A couple of months later, Bill and Dan moved into their huge fixer-upper. But unfortunately, it was the beginning of the end. Through the years I had often worked with couples who were either remodeling or building. The ordeal added so much stress to their relationship that things never quite went back to being the same once the project was completed. This was the case for Bill and Dan.

Bill was anxious to have everything perfect and he was willing to work on the house every spare minute, day or night. Dan, on the other hand, missed the social life that they had forfeited since Bill's purchase. Just going to a movie or out to dinner with friends took a back seat to working on the house – on Bill's house. That was the crux of the matter. It was Bill's house and no matter how many times he told Dan differently, Dan knew whose name was on the deed.

In time the house became presentable but it would never, ever be finished. There was always just one more thing that needed to be done, one more project to tackle. Dan worked with Bill, or for Bill, in the catering and then in his off time, worked with Bill, or for Bill, on the house – and it was a big house. In fact, Bill had decided to rent out the upstairs as an apartment, which brought in extra income but also took away some of their privacy. Renters would come and go to the point that I stopped making an effort to learn their names.

One evening I stopped by their home to check on things but quickly saw that they were too busy and in foul moods. I said goodbye and ran into the latest tenant coming in as I was leaving.

"Are they fighting again?" he asked.

"What? No," I replied. But I was curious and asked, "Do they fight often?"

"Oh Lord, yes. Practically nightly," the young man said. "I hear things being thrown and yelling. They have kept me up all night on more than one occasion. I don't know how much more that I can take."

"I am sorry. I did not know," I said sadly.

"It's bad, really bad," he added as he ascended the outside stairs to his apartment.

I called Bill a few days later and invited him to lunch. At first he was about to make an excuse but then relented. We met at a favorite neighborhood spot.

"Everything okay?" I asked.

"Sure, why wouldn't it be?" he replied, looking concerned.

"It's just that I hear you and Dan have been fighting some."

"Who said that?" he bristled. "The jerk I rented the upstairs to? He's making it up." But after a pause, he continued, "Sure, we have had some disagreements but all couples do."

"Bill, this is me. I know you. Love you. And I worry about you. Talk to me."

"It's bad," he said looking away from me. "I can't make him happy anymore. And I think that he is seeing someone."

"When would he have time? He is either working with you in the catering business or working with you on the house," I said.

"True," Bill said with a shrug. "But he just seems so distant."

"You two need to have some fun," I suggested.

"A midnight run?" he asked.

"No, I mean fun that won't get you arrested," I replied with a smile.

"I don't think I remember how."

Two weeks later Bill ended up in the emergency room with a broken jaw. Dan called me and I came running. He was so upset, saying that he did not mean to do it, but that Bill just wouldn't let up – that he had kept yelling at him. Bill had accused Dan of being unfaithful.

"Ricky, I have been faithful to Bill for nearly 15 years," Dan confided. "Yes, I played around at first, but I wasn't ready to settle down right after getting out of the awful mess that I was in when I met him. I told him so and then I asked him why he would even think that. He got so mad and pushed me, and then I pushed back. He tried to hit me but missed. I should have walked away. But instead, I hit back and broke his jaw. The doctor said that he will have to have it wired shut. I never meant to do it."

I was so furious with Dan that I could hardly be civil to him. And yet, he was also in pain. I loved both of them and found myself conflicted with emotions. How could I kick Dan when he was already down?

Bill looked rough and was drugged when we brought him home. I wasn't sure what to think or believe. But surprisingly Bill was not mad.

"It's not his fault. I started it," Bill mumbled through clenched teeth.

Bill, for whatever reason, did not blame him.

It felt like years, although it was just a few months, before Bill had the wires removed. Dan had to turn every meal into a milkshake for him. I know that I am being petty but this is the part that I hated the most: Bill lost over twenty pounds in the process. Almost enough to make me want to ask Dan to pop me in the jaw, too. And in typical Bill fashion, he had to point out how his clothes were falling off of him. Nothing fit. Trust me when I say it was hard as hell to feel any empathy for him — the skinny evil bitch!

—•—

A couple of years later, I bought a house, too. It was in the neighborhood near Bill and Dan and like their home, it was definitely a fixer-upper. My go-to contractor for design jobs was inundated with work, and while I appreciated his honesty, I was disappointed when he suggested that I find someone else to work on my home. I hired a guy referred to me by a neighbor but it was a disastrous relationship. He kept having excuses for this and that, while at the same time offering hard-luck stories.

Even though I knew better, I would pay in advance for work to be done. It did not take me long to realize that I was being taken advantage of and that I needed to put an end to it. The whole situation made me very receptive when a realtor contacted me and said that she had someone interested if I would consider selling. I did not hesitate for a minute to resell after only a few months, and buy another house in better condition on "my" side of town.

I used a couple of the downstairs rooms in my new home for my office and sample room and I lived primarily on the second floor. I was finally able to eliminate my storage unit and fill my new home with the treasures that I had collected over the years. Occasionally, I would move a piece or two through my design business but for the most part, I was able to make everything work in my own home.

All of my "boys" were doing small jobs every now and then. I know Bill and Dan picked up an assortment of patio furniture from a condominium clubhouse one night. I appreciated that they asked me if I needed anything and if I wanted to help. But I declined.

Greg was known to shoplift small items at furniture stores, including Palmer's during their going out of business sale. Like all of us, Greg did not need anything but I think he just enjoyed the thrill of getting away with something.

Dean moved out and in with another girlfriend but Greg was fine with that, and I think he enjoyed having the place all to himself again. I was worried that Dean would want a lot of the things Greg had acquired while they lived together but he actually took very little. A few months later we heard that he had married for a second time but none of us received an invitation to his wedding.

As for Leon, I had no idea of what or who he was doing. For a few years after our breakup, I would hear things or run into him at parties of mutual friends. But then it was like he had vanished. I did not lose sleep over not knowing the details. My biggest concern with all of them was that they might get careless and be caught. And just having one of us arrested could easily bring down all of us. I never felt that anyone, including me, would hold up well under interrogation. We were all connected by our past transgressions. I was grateful that no one ever felt the need to use that to their advantage.

One morning, while having my coffee and reading the newspaper obituaries, I saw that Dean had died. It took my breath away. He was only 42 and left behind his second wife and a child that I never knew he had fathered. I immediately called Greg and asked if he was aware of Dean's death and if so, did he know what had happened. He was as shocked as I was and said that he would try to find out details.

I thought back to our college days when Greg, Dean and I lived together in our avocado-carpeted town house with a mash-up of dorm furniture and pieces from our families. Dean was my very first roommate and for many years he would move in and out of my life. I regretted that for the last several years, he had been out of my life and my thoughts. He was Nathaniel and the Midnight Movers' lone straight man, although he had been known to dip his toe in the sissy pool on more than one occasion.

Greg called a mutual friend of his and Dean's who said that Dean had been dealing with heart issues for some time. Combined with drinking and stress, it had finally taken its toll. None of us knew anything about that until now, when Dean's heart finally gave out. I felt such guilt for losing touch with him. I never thought that the last time I saw him would be the final time.

I called Bill and told him the news and that Greg and I had planned to go to the funeral. He said that he wanted to join us and would ask Dan as well.

"I am going to try to find Leon," I said. "I doubt that he would want to come. But I just think letting him know is the right thing to do."

"Good luck," Bill said sincerely.

I called the last number that I had for Leon but it had been disconnected. I tried his work number, not knowing if he was even still employed. The woman who answered said she did not know anyone there by that name.

I got into my car and rode over to his rental house and knocked on the door. A young woman with a baby in her arms answered but was of no help as well. She said that she and her husband had been renting that house for the past eight months and had no idea of who had lived there before them. Had it really been so long since I had talked with or seen Leon?

I still had a number for Freddy at home and decided that I would try him.

"Hello."

"Freddy, it's Ricky. You know, Leon's Ricky."

"What's up?"

"Do you have a number for Leon?" I asked. "Do you know where he is?"

"He moved back home last year and yes, I have his number but I am not comfortable giving it to you," said Freddy coolly.

I thought to myself: *What had Leon said about me? I am sure that I am the bad guy in his scenario, but was I bad enough to now be kept from talking to him? It did not make any sense to me.*

"Freddy, a mutual friend of ours has died and I thought Leon might want to know."

"I can give him a message and ask him to call you."

I wanted to be the one to tell Leon, not Freddy. I gave him my number and asked that he pass it along to Leon. I was surprised that Freddy was not even curious enough to ask who had died. But then he had rarely focused on anything other than himself.

The funeral was in three days and Bill, Dan, Greg and I rode together. The casket was closed and I was disappointed because I wanted to see my old friend one more time. His wife was cordial when we introduced ourselves and offered our condolences. She said, "I know all about the four of you. Dean had lots of stories."

It was a simple service conducted by a preacher who clearly did not know Dean. There was nothing personal in the words that he spoke.

Once we were back in the car, I repeated what Dean's wife had said.

"She knows all about us... Dean told her lots of stories."

"I thought about that all through the service," said Bill. "What do you think she knows?"

"I can't imagine that Dean would tell her any Nathaniel stories," added Greg.

"Maybe not, but didn't you say that he had been drinking a lot? Remember how chatty Leon would get with his stories when he drank?" questioned Dan.

The four of us sat in silence for a mile or two until Greg asked. "Why didn't Leon come?"

"I don't know. He never called me back," I said. "But it would have be a long drive for him and he has been out of our lives for some time." I then added, "Plus, he never really spent that much time around Dean."

"But we are all connected to each other, whether we want to be or not," Greg said emotionally. "We are *Nathaniel and the Midnight Movers* dammit!"

—•—

Six months after Dean's funeral, Dan moved out. I thought that he and Bill had worked things out and had been getting along better, but clearly I was wrong. Although there were still things to do with the house, it had no longer consumed them. The catering business had been thriving and they had hired extra hands to help. Still, I know that sometimes when a relationship goes to extreme resentment, fighting and injury, it is hard to find the love and kindness that it once had.

Bill said that he had suspected it would eventually happen but had kept hoping to be able to make things right. For Dan, not only was he giving up his home, but he also walked away from his job.

And even though they had been together for nearly fifteen years, Bill's shrew of a sister made the point of saying that she knew it wouldn't work from the beginning.

"He was always taking advantage of you and I never did trust him or like him. I can't believe that you put up with him, especially after that broken jaw incident. He should have been arrested and thrown in jail," she said as venom dripped from each word.

"Shut up. Just shut the hell up," Bill said softly and calmly with each word measured and precise. Then he stared her down. I was so glad to have been present and able to witness that miracle. I wanted to stand up and yell, break out my pompoms and lead a cheer. However, I could tell that she was not done but as she opened her mouth to speak, Bill looked at her with disgust and stopped her dead in her tracks with one word.

"Don't."

Dan had been with Bill on each and every midnight run and had been an equal partner in the take-a-turn selection with each nightly haul. Therefore, the removal of Dan's possessions left a sizable dent in Bill's furnishings. Plus, Dan took a catering manager's job at one of Bill's competitors. And yet, Bill did not put up a fight or get angry. He knew it was time and he still loved Dan so much that he had no intention of hurting him or resisting. Because of that, Dan was not greedy or vengeful. It was a very sad yet amicable separation. I loved them both dearly and did not want to lose either one of them from my life. I hoped that neither would make me choose or test my loyalty.

Dan rented a small apartment and I offered to help him arrange his furnishings and decorate. I told Bill that I was planning to do that. I did not ask for his permission but was grateful all the same when he thanked me for helping Dan.

"The same offer goes for you, too," I said. "We can rearrange and fluff and make everything fresh and new." He thanked me and asked that I give him a little more time to adjust to the emptiness. I realized then that Bill was not ready to erase any remaining signs of Dan being a part of his home or a part of his life.

Chapter Twenty-One

As my interior design business continued to grow, more and more opportunities came my way – including being asked, for the first time, to be the designer for one of the model homes for the infamous annual Home Tour. There were eight homes that year, once again built side by side on a cul-de-sac in a new cluster home development. My builder was gay and appreciated the dramatic. While others chose to take the safe route, I met with absolutely no resistance when I suggested several over-the-top ideas.

I was anxious to take a look at the other model homes during the opening night party because I had walked through several of the houses while under construction. However, once they neared completion and furnishings started going in, everyone became very protective of their projects and it was a definite no-no to go snooping.

I was very proud of our house and what we had achieved. Unlike several of the furniture stores who participated, I did not have an unlimited source for furnishings. I pulled from what I had on hand (that had not been stolen) and then asked my design clients if I could borrow one of their tables or lamps. Everyone was thrilled to be asked, thinking that I thought their piece was special enough to be included in the prestigious home tour.

The opening night party was elegant and included the builders and their associates, the designers and vendors along with selected guests, and definitely the media. Judges had been through the homes earlier in the day and had decided on the award-winners. I would have loved *Best of Show* but knew that I had taken a risk in being so extreme with my design. It was going to be a love-it or hate-it situation. When all was said and done, I did receive the award for *Best Master Suite* so I did not go home empty handed. Plus, the builder was thrilled and already had a contract on the house. Clearly, we must have done something right.

As I toured the other models, I was surprised by the mediocrity of a couple of the entries. Some homes had a few things that I thought were striking and innovative but overall, there was a lot of safe and barely average. However, the winner of *Best of Show* was spectacular and deserving of the award. The house itself had a stately exterior and a dramatic floor plan with two-story rooms and balcony overlooks. I had been anxious to see the furnishings because of the pre-tour article. Yes, they had completed their house first and snapped up the early press.

After seeing the article, Bill asked – and I don't think that he was joking – if I would like to do a pre-tour run around midnight one night.

"Hell, no," I said firmly.

We were now into the 1990s and security alarms and nightly patrols had become commonplace. Having my own tour home, for the first time, caused me to go to my dark thoughts as I realized, that someone could break into my model home. And since many of the pieces were on loan from clients, it would be a huge debacle. It could ruin me.

According to the newspaper article, there was a new furniture store about to open and they were involved with the award-winning design. There was so much in that house that I would have loved to have owned, whether legitimately or by way of a midnight run with my best friends – my crew. Curious, I opened a drawer here and there and saw the furniture manufactures brands and realized that many of the lines had been carried years ago by the late and great Palmer's Fine Furniture.

I was excited that this new store would be offering the exclusive lines that Palmer's had sold for many years. Then across the room I saw a familiar face. It was the jackass husband of the Palmer's daughter. The jerk who insulted and dismissed me when I applied for a job all those years ago. What was that douchebag's name? I remember that his wife kept her maiden name of Palmer, but what was his name?

And then, I noticed the stack of brochures sitting on the chest in the entrance hall. They were advertising the new store, Howard's Fine Furniture. Howard's? That was *his* name. This must be *his* store. It finally sank in that these furnishings were from *his* store.

I walked over to what's-his-name Howard and introduced myself. I congratulated him on his award, and in turn, he congratulated me on my master bedroom win.

"Didn't you use to run Palmer's Fine Furniture a few years back?" I asked, although I already knew the answer.

"Yes, it was my wife's company. Well, her family's store and she inherited it," he replied.

"It was always one of my favorite places to shop. My parents as well. I was so sorry to see it close," I said with all the sincerity that I could muster.

"It got to the point that no one wanted fine furniture. But I am happy to say that the tide is changing. There seem to be people out there wanting something of quality again. Or, at least I am banking on it," he explained.

I needed to prod more. Since he clearly did not remember me, I continued.

"Didn't Palmer's do a home tour years ago? And I think I remember seeing your things in some condominium models as well," I asked.

"If only we had stayed out of the model business. But my wife thought that it would be good exposure for the store.

The only exposure that it gained us was the attention of some thieving bastards who cleaned us out. First it was a condo model here and another one there. The police told us that in addition to our losses, the thieves also hit a few other places that, fortunately, we were not involved with. Still, the one that about put us under was that tour home. Because of that, I almost said no to being involved with this tour. And yet, with a new business starting up, I decided that we needed to take advantage of the thousands of people who will come through."

"So what happened with that tour home, if you don't mind me asking?"

"We were all set for a photo shoot and advance publicity but the night before it was scheduled we were robbed. It must have been a big professional crew with moving trucks although no one ever admitted to seeing anything. They cleaned us out. I had even expressed concern a few days earlier with the builder about putting in an alarm. He said that he would get around to it but he didn't do it before the break-in. Those guys must have been watching us, or at the very least, were extremely lucky. They hit us on the first night that everything was in and set up."

I found myself getting nervous and knew that I should have walked away. But I just couldn't.

"Do you know if they ever caught them?" I inquired.

"No, we kept thinking pieces would come back on the market, show up somewhere. But they never did. They must have taken them out of state or something. Wait, I take that back, they did make an effort to arrest someone once who tried to sell something in a consignment shop that matched the description of a piece that was stolen from us – a rattan table with a unique butterfly laminate top. When they asked where he got the table, all he could come up with was from 'a friend of a friend,' so they let him go. They did not have enough evidence to hold him."

"Wow, that is amazing," I said, remembering so well that table and the blackmailing neighbors who it had belonged to.

"And the thing is, the police said that there had been a whole string of robberies over the years and even a few close calls where they almost caught them. However, there were so many burglaries that they were not even sure if they were all connected. They did not know if it was one crew or several crews. But the one thing that the police were sure about was that the thieves were professionals. I agree that they must have been pros. Just because of the sheer volume of everything they took, how often they hit and the fact that they never got caught."

He then added, "You better make sure your tour home's alarm gets turned on tonight. I don't know if the thieves are still out there, but I know that I am not taking any chances."

I was finally seeing this from the other side. No longer as the thief but as the potential victim. None of us ever knew all of the ramifications felt from our heists. We never knew the consequences from our actions or how it might have affected someone personally or financially.

I apologized for monopolizing his time on such a busy night and again offered my congratulations. I told him that I was looking forward to the opening of Howard's Fine Furniture.

Chapter Twenty-Two
present Day

"You did what?" Bill asked in disbelief. "You never told me that story."

"I didn't want you to have a nervous breakdown. I figured you would love to know that we were being talked about, but that you would think that I was being careless in getting that close to the fire."

"You are correct on both counts," Bill said with a grin. "Professional crew, huh? I am not sure if we were ever really professional or just damn lucky. And you say that the police never knew for sure if all of the robberies were connected? I would love to see their list of our greatest hits, even if it was just to remind me of some of the jobs that I may have forgotten."

"Bill, we have known each for nearly 40 years now. Would you have ever thought that we would still be here talking about this?" I asked.

"It is amazing. But seriously," he said gesturing to the sale items, "you know that you are going to miss all of this. Life will be so dull without all of your pretties."

"I will always have pretties, Bill. In fact, with the money from this sale, I will go buy some things to make my new place wonderful. I will shop around and choose just the right pieces. I won't have to make my choices from whatever store or designer was responsible for decorating a furnished model, no matter how spectacular they were."

"You know, I was surprised when you got rid of everything at your parents' home after your mother died," said Bill, catching me off guard.

"What did I need? I kept a couple of family pieces but other than that, it was time to let it all go," I said. "Although — funny that you brought it up — the one thing that I still regret not keeping was that Hepplewhite console in their entrance hall. It was the first piece of furniture that I picked up. Remember, I told you about that. I was just sixteen with a brand new driver's license. My first 'Midnight' job."

"And you stored everything in the attic of some church friends, right?" said Bill, continuing my story.

"Yes. I also got a Stiffel lamp and an octagon-shaped commode table — a style from the 1960s that didn't really hold up over the years. But that console was timeless. And my mother always loved it."

"I was surprised that you weren't at your parents' estate sale," Bill said.

"How did you know? Were you there?" I asked and Bill nodded. "I had a different company helping me with that sale and they were insistent that I not be there. And it was just as well. I had an emotional attachment to the things there that I have never felt with what I have now. Again, if I had any regrets, it would be not keeping that console."

"You can come visit it if you want to," Bill offered.

"What do you mean?" I asked.

"I'm the one who bought it. It's in my upstairs hallway."

"How did I not know that?" Dumbfounded, I asked. "Seriously?"

"You never go upstairs. Hell, I rarely go up there myself. But it is there and if you want it back, you may have it."

I thanked him and told him "No." But I was happy to learn that was still in the family.

"I also picked up a bunch of silver serving pieces that are now tarnishing away in my butler's pantry. I remember overhearing someone ask at your sale if the family who lived there were caterers. I butted in and told them 'No, they were entertainers.' Your parents loved to give parties, but then, so did you at one time."

"What about you?" I asked. "You love parties."

"No, I don't. For me, who actually worked in the catering business for years, parties are just work – a job."

"At least you taught Dan well," I added. "Do you know if he is still a catering manager?"

"No, I don't know. I haven't heard from him in a couple of years now," Bill said with a tinge of sadness. "We used to talk now and then, but not anymore."

"I am so sorry. You stayed together a long time. Longer than Leon and me."

"No one could live with you for long," he replied in typical Bill fashion.

"Bitch," I said, smiling sweetly.

"You know it!"

—•—

"Hey there, I'm sorry to interrupt," Roberta Ann said, entering the kitchen. "But we're winding down and bringing the unsold pieces back inside."

"Do you need some help?" I asked.

"No, we can handle it. You two looked deep in conversation—I'm sorry I barged in. Enjoy your coffee and let us do our thing," she replied.

"Are you pleased with everything?" I asked

"What he means is, did he make any money?" Bill added with a chuckle.

"Oh my, yes! This was one of the most successful sales that I've ever done. I already know the figures from yesterday but will total everything up tonight and let you know the final amount tomorrow, if that's okay with you," she said. "You'll be able to comfortably furnish your new place in the grand style that you're accustomed to."

"And without having to lift a thing!" Bill said with a smirk.

Roberta Ann smiled and excused herself. For the next twenty minutes we heard her and the girls moving things around. And then she tapped on the door, cracked it open a bit, said her goodbyes and promised to settle up the next day.

—•—

Bill and I sat there for a while in silence — each of us truly comfortable, feeling no need to talk. Just a couple of old friends who, together, had been through so much. A couple of old friends who could just sit and appreciate the quiet.

" You do realize that we are the final two," Bill said with a faraway look.

"No, Dean is the only one who has passed away. Leon is probably somewhere still drunk on his ass. And we know that Greg is okay — I mean, even though he moved to the west coast, I still hear from him regularly. Also, I am sure that Dan is doing fine, too. But yes, people do move on and things change. However, you and I, we are still here. In spite of everything. We are still standing."

"Barely. You with your arthritic knees and me with my new hip," Bill said in his typical smart-ass way.

"Regardless," I said smiling. "I can't imagine my life without you — you tired old piece."

"Nathaniel, you old sweet-talker. You always could tell a convincing lie."

Made in the USA
Columbia, SC
28 May 2019